STYX

ALSO BY NIKITA GILL

Hekate

Animal Tales from India

Wild Embers

Fierce Fairytales

The Girl and the Goddess

These are the Words

Where Hope Comes From

Great Goddesses

STYX

THE RIVER

NIKITA GILL

solstice

London · New York · Amsterdam/Antwerp · Sydney/Melbourne · Toronto · New Delhi

First published in Great Britain by Solstice Books, an imprint of Simon & Schuster UK Ltd, 2026
Simultaneously published in US by Little, Brown and Company,
a division of Hachette Book Group, Inc, 2026

1 3 5 7 9 10 8 6 4 2

Simon & Schuster UK Ltd, 7th Floor,
199 Bishopsgate, Broadgate, London EC2M 3TY

Simon & Schuster Australia, Sydney
Simon & Schuster India, New Delhi

www.simonandschuster.co.uk
www.simonandschuster.com.au
www.simonandschuster.co.in

The authorised representative in the EEA is Simon & Schuster Netherlands BV, Herculesplein 96, 3584 AA Utrecht, Netherlands. info@simonandschuster.nl

A CIP catalogue record for this book is available from the British Library

Hardback ISBN: 978-1-3985-3719-4
Trade Paperback ISBN: 978-1-3985-3720-0
eBook ISBN: 978-1-3985-3721-7
Audio ISBN: 978-1-3985-3722-4

Map by Robert Lazzaretti

Typeset in Perpetua by M Rules
Printed and Bound in the UK using 100% Renewable Electricity at CPI Group (UK) Ltd

FSC www.fsc.org
MIX
Paper | Supporting responsible forestry
FSC® C013604

For you who
is half star, half ocean.
I hope you find the sisterhood
you have always wished for.

ATLAS GARDENS
CRIUS & EURYBIA'S PALACE
TETHYS TOWER
OCEANUS' PALACE
STYX & ASTERIA'S CAVE
COEUS & PHOEBE'S PALACE
KRONOS & RHEA'S PALACE
CRETE

WHERE THE DAY
AND
NIGHT FEAST
MAINLAND
TARTARUS
VOLCANOE
MOUTH OF THE
UNDERWORLD
OCEANUS'

Dramatis Personae

Styx	Oldest of the Oceanids, firstborn Titan child of Oceanus and Tethys
Asteria	Goddess of Oracles and Falling Stars
Oceanus	The Great River, father of the Oceanids and River Gods, oldest Titan brother
Tethys	Goddess of Fresh Water, Titanide, consort of Oceanus, mother to Oceanids and River Gods
Kronos	God-King of the Titans
Rhea	Wife of Kronos, mother to the Olympians
Perses	God of Destruction
Pallas	God of Warcraft
Coeus	God of Intellect, Titan, father to Asteria and Leto
Phoebe	Goddess of Prophecy and Light, Titanide, mother to Asteria and Leto
Metis	Goddess of Wisdom and Cunning
Leto	Goddess of Motherhood and Childbirth, sister of Asteria and daughter of Coeus and Phoebe
Crius	God of Constellations, father of Pallas and Perses
Eurybia	Goddess of the Power, mother of Pallas and Perses
Zeus	God of Thunder and Lightning, Olympian, son of Kronos and Rhea
Hyperion	God of Light
Gaia	The earth, mother of Titans, Primordial God
Nyx	Goddess of the Night, Primordial God
Tartarus	The abyss and volcano, Primordial God
Others	Three thousand Oceanids, three thousand River Gods

The Age of Titans

Before the rule of the Olympians, before the tale of Zeus and Hera and their powerful siblings, there were the *Titans*.

A golden era of divinity when the earth was still new.

Back then, there was no hierarchy because divinity engulfed all who were celestial – there were simply Gods and Goddesses, no one was lesser than the other.

For a time, there was a sacred peace. However, desire for power is a corrupting force. When the youngest Titan son, Kronos, declared himself king of the Gods after defeating his own father, Ouranos, by butchering him and excommunicating him – a new order was born.

And in every hierarchy there are those who are relegated to the lowest rung. In this story, these were the lesser Goddesses who lost their godhood and were instead named nymphs.

But Goddesses are an ancient force answerable to no one. This is a story of a nymph who fought the odds.

The story of a nymph who became a God.

Styx

A CHILD MADE OF SEA GLASS AND SPITE

PART I

I Think I Was Born from My Parents' Rage

Back when they were simply
the oldest of the Titans
caught under the cruel rule

of a father that controlled both sky
and their own mother Gaia,
the entire earth at his cruel whim.

What else could explain my split eyes,
the poison green of my hair,
and my two serpentlike fangs?

Back before everything shattered,
this was no terrible thing.
In fact, I was born deeply loved.

My birth was one of great rejoicing.
I was the first child of the Titans,
the rulers of a bright new realm.

After my aunts drew me from my mother's womb
and washed me with fresh waters
taken from her favourite lake,

my father crafted a hurricane
and blessed it with my name.
My uncle Hyperion gave me jewels

made from amber rays taken from the sun.
I was heralded as a new beginning,
born from the bloodshed they no longer

wanted to think of, an unnamed atrocity.
So when I was passed from Titanide to Titan,
it was like I was the trophy that had been won.

Until I reached my grandmother, Gaia,
maker of this earth, who refused to hold me.
Instead, she stared at me, tiny, in my mother's arms

and whispered, like a premonition,
'She will never be beautiful.
One day, this will be her ruin.'

I defied this prophecy.
In the end, I defied everything
my family expected of me.

Genesis

Before my birth,
there were my parents:
oldest of twelve golden Titans
born of my grandmother Gaia's womb.

My father, Oceanus,
was the Great River
that surrounded
Gaia's whole earth.

It would be from his great river
that every sea and ocean
and lake and river
would be born.

And my mother, Tethys,
was the Goddess
of Fresh Water that nourished
the forests and animals

on Gaia's green earth.
Before the Titans,
it had been Gaia and Ouranos,
the great sky, that ruled over all.

But power is a slow poison.
Ouranos was unhappy
having to share rulership with Gaia,
who had been more than his consort.

She was also his maker.
In his quest for solitary dominance,
Ouranos committed a terrible outrage
against Gaia and her children.

And in return, my youngest uncle,
Kronos, the God of Time,
usurped his father's throne
to teach him a lesson.

Still, Gaia wept for her consort.
She wept for what was lost
inside the mouth of vengeance.
It was grief which led her

to speak her words about me.
Grief that curdled
her premonition
into my curse.

My Father Was So Furious

on hearing Gaia's words, he took me into his arms
and carried me away to the golden sands:
tiny quartz crystals that had developed
under the weather and wear of his oceans.

He walked with me for hours
until his favourite brother, Coeus,
God of Intellect, was sent to calm him
and bring us home. 'Styx is loved by many,'

Coeus told him, 'but no one
needs to be loved by all.
And our mother is still grieving.
She will love her too in time.'

Oceanus's sea-green eyes stormed
and his long, sea-foam-white beard
trembled with anger as he spoke.
'A child is no place to put misspent grief.'

My uncle studied the waves
of the ocean my father had so lovingly crafted
with his own two hands. 'Gaia is a law
unto herself. You cannot change her.'

My father looked down at me
and kissed my forehead.
'Perhaps not. But I can protect
my children from her influence.'

Perhaps my father had meant these words then.
Perhaps he did not know himself to be
the God that I have come to know him to be.
I would like to think he *wanted* to protect me.

I would like to think that he did not know
that some promises are an undoing
in and of themselves.
That they are not meant for even Gods to keep.

Back Then

Oceanus's palace was still new,
a beating sapphire jewel
in the heart of Gaia's earth.

His great river's waters,
which eventually became
the seven seas and five oceans,

ran azure, cerulean, turquoise,
every shade of lazuline blue
you can imagine under the sky

all around the palace.
My father had built
his chambers above ground,

the floors made of thick,
impenetrable diamond glass,
just transparent enough

for us to see the waters below.
Imagine an impossible island palace
full of the banks

of this great river,
not far from the golden
shores of his first ocean.

It was a lonely place at first,
for my grandmother's
premonition stopped my parents

from having any more children.
I spent a childhood alone,
playing with oysters and dolphins.

My mother would brush my long,
poison-green locks
and tell me stories

about the silver fish
and sea creatures
that surrounded our palace.

I wish I could say I missed company
but you do not miss
what you do not know.

It was only when my uncles
and aunts began to create
their own progeny

that my parents thought
to make me brothers
and sisters.

It was only when they met
their nieces and nephews
that they realized

they had made
a terrible mistake
with me.

I Was the First of My Kind

The children of Gods
were meant to be Gods.
This law was established
by Kronos in the infancy of his rule,

a reign that was born
after my own birth.
Other than my strange appearance,
I had shown no powers

all through my childhood.
No one knew then
that the way to bless
children with divine powers

was to determine their gifts
from the moment they were born.
It was Kronos who created
the ritual of blessing our children.

It was under his decree
our favours were given to us.
Our fathers were meant to put
their hands to our heads,

bless us with the knowledge
of what Gods are meant to do.
I had received no such blessing,
so the name for what I was did not yet exist.

Oceanid

It was my mother who thought up the name.
I remember it well, for it was the last time
she was not pregnant.

I had been a singular child running through
this diamond and ocean palace
for an untold era now, happy in my solitude.

But I had overheard my parents speaking
of their nephews and nieces,
how it would be good for me

if I was not the only one of my kind.
'Styx is already strange,' my father had said.
'I do not wish for her to be alone.'

Perhaps I was becoming too unruly
even for my father's old promise.
Too much for his comforts.

That day, Tethys walked into my father's
underground chambers, the wings on her brow beating
as they always did when she was deep in thought,

and her long fingers wrapped around
my small, still plump hand, keeping me from running.
She said, 'I have seen a vision.'

My father, who was crafting
a particularly tricky sea, looked up
to his wife, her silver curls flowing freely.

'What did you see?' All Titans knew to take
visions as prophecies now. Especially
after what had happened to Ouranos.

'I saw your riverbanks full of children,
laughter everywhere in these gilded halls.'
My mother had a glow of pride as she said this.

My father stopped working.
'How many children?' he asked softly.
My mother's smile widened.

'Countless children, oh king of oceans,
further than my eyes could see.'
My father's smile was like the sea

when the sun fell on its waters.
His eyes glittered like jewels
as he gazed at my mother.

'You could not bestow me
with a greater gift, my queen.'
She nodded in return, her eyes misty.

They had wanted this a long time.
A vision was like permission for our kind.
'Your sons are to be known as the Potamoi,'

my mother continued, 'and your daughters
will be Oceanids, named after their powerful father.'
I saw a change in Oceanus in every word spoken.

His demeanour softened, the rigidity
with which he carried himself relaxed.
He walked toward my mother and pulled her

into an embrace. Her hand left mine
in that moment. It seems so strange
to think back to it now.

The way her hand left mine.
The way she never held it
with that kind of love again.

I Realized I Did Not Like That Word, *Oceanid*

When you name something,
are you naming it because you love it?

Or are you naming it to build it a golden cage
of your understanding?

Names can do that.
They can become a drowning.

They can grow around your wrists
and shackle you to their meaning.

When I walked away
from my father's chambers

I realized my hands
were clenched into fists.

I did not want to be an Oceanid,
one of countless sisters.

I wanted to be like my parents.
I wanted powers of my very own.

An Uneasy Reign

Although my father was the oldest
of all the Titan Gods,
it was Kronos,
the youngest of the Titan brothers,
who had overthrown Ouranos.

This meant that the throne,
the leadership of the Titan realms,
were all under Kronos's rule.
He was not just a God,
he was *king* of the Gods.

One evening I heard
my uncle Hyperion, God of Light,
speaking with my father.
I was always listening back then.
A lonely palace has many hiding places,

and my favourite was the large sapphire rock
I could fit behind just next to my father's chambers
where his river flowed so softly underfoot.
I could hear everything.
No one had told me I could not, but I still hid.

'Rhea is pregnant,' Hyperion said.
'But the prophecy from Ouranos
lingers long on Kronos's mind and crown.'
My father's heavy, deep voice replied,
'Then he must learn to wear the crown better.'

Hyperion's voice lowered to a whisper:
'Brother, you know as well as I
that Kronos is the most . . . volatile

one of us all. I fear that—'
My father's voice was coral-edge sharp.

'Hyperion. Kronos is king.
We never spoke. Do you understand?'
I did not hear my uncle's response,
but I heard his footsteps leaving.
A question wormed its way into my mind.

What prophecy were they talking about?

Brothers Before Sisters

It was my brothers
who were born next
of my mother's womb.

By then, I was old enough
to help with their births
alongside my aunts.

I had grown from
an unruly and free childhood
into a more wary girlhood.

Every birth after my own
happened in multiples.
Like the fish she nurtured,

my mother gave birth
to schools of children.
Five brothers arrived at once.

My aunts and I had just
enough hands to catch
and wash them all.

While the women worked,
the male Gods celebrated
with cups full of nectar.

Theirs was an easy task.
To get drunk, eat well,
and simply wait.

I resented their laughter,
their easy conversation
while my mother laboured

and my aunts and I
held her hands,
cooled her forehead,

helped her through
the difficult task
of birthing new life.

It was a messy act,
bringing children
into this world.

All that ichor,
the golden Gods' blood,
that was spilled,

my mother's screams
as the tiny bodies
of my crying brothers arrived.

I shuddered as I lifted
one of them up.
He gazed up at me

with clear green irises.
He looked more
like my parents

than I ever had.

After That My Mother Was Always Pregnant

Gone were the days
where she brushed my hair
and sung me lullabies.

Gone were the moments
where she joined me for walks
on the golden sands at sunset.

I saw so little of her now.
She spent most of her time
with my aunts, talking about children,

while my brothers grew craggy
like the cliffs they played on,
hands like bedrock.

None of them wanted
to play with an older sister,
which suited me.

I liked the pleasure
of my own company.
But late at night

while my brothers
snored in their rooms,
growing the way divinity grows,

quickly, quicker than me.
I would put my arms
around myself in my bed,

trying to remember
what my mother's embrace
felt like back

when I was her only child.
Back when it was just
her and me.

The Potamoi

My brothers looked a little like me.
Some were born with ivory bull horns
or with the golden tails of fish.

Others had bodies made of sea rock.
Some even had sharp fangs
and looked even more serpentine than me.

Yet while my features were considered
graceless, or even, as I had overheard
an unkind aunt say, *Styx is so unsightly*,

I had noticed how differently
my brothers were treated.
Despite their strange features,

no one whispered about their horns,
their tails, their coarseness.
It was only after they were born that I realized

that even though I was merely tolerated
for looking nothing like the vivid-eyed,
elegant beauty of my mother and aunts,

my brothers were celebrated
for their peculiar features, which were nothing
like the light that exuded from my father

and all his many brothers.

My Father Did Not Change

At least not then and not toward me.
Where my mother barely had time
to glance my way anymore,

my father did his best to make
an effort to carve moments with me.
Of course, he was preoccupied.

Crafting oceans and seas
and teaching his sons
the rules of godhood

took up much of his time.
But one day when I sat alone
on the sands watching his ocean's

cerulean waters
devour the orange glow
of a setting sun,

he came to find me.
'Styx,' he said warmly,
'my eldest child.

Why are you here alone?
You should bring your brothers
with you. They will keep you company.'

By now my brothers
were so numerous
it was hard to count them all.

I shook my head.
'I prefer the silence here.'
The palace had become too chaotic for me.

I had caught my youngest brothers
going through my chambers
and running away with

my favourite oyster-shell comb,
and stealing the jewels I had collected
from the seas, much to my outrage and anger.

'I know this has been difficult.'
Oceanus lowered himself
to the warm sands next to me.

'But you must know
your mother and I
treasure you as our eldest.'

Instead of saying petulantly,
It does not feel that way,
I kept my eyes trained on the sun.

'Styx, you must know
as the oldest child
of the oldest Gods,

you are a herald
of a brand-new age.'
I could not stop myself.

When he said these words
my acerbic tongue sprang to life.
'Are all heralds powerless, Father?

Am I meant to be the only one
with no gifts to speak of?'
He gazed at me troubled, before saying,

'Your brothers do not
have such fine gifts either, Styx.'
I glared at him.

'You blessed each of them
to become a God of your rivers, Father.
Does that not count as a gift?'

I saw the dangerous storm
start to swirl in his eyes.
But then he closed them and said,

'Oceanids will gain consorts
and through them,
you will find power.

And as my eldest,
you will gain the most power,
more than you realize.

But the Potamoi must
look after themselves.'
I seethed at his words.

'Is that all I am made for?
To be a symbol of status for a consort
and never have anything of my own?'

My father sighed
and rested his hand on my head.
'You are destined for more

than you ever dreamed of.
Be patient, my child.
You do not know

what the future holds,
only the Fates do.'
There was something

about the way he spoke,
his voice low and rumbling
like an oncoming hurricane.

He knew something about me
that I was unaware of.
Something even my mother

did not yet know.

The Arrival of My Sisters

Each time I was summoned
to my mother's chambers for a new birth,
I saw fewer aunts than before.
In my childish naivety
I thought that this was because
all immortals delivered easily.

But it was because my mother simply
kept on giving birth;
perpetually there was a fresh new son
nursing at her bosom,
until my father gave her the title
of the Goddess of Nursing too.

That day when I was summoned to her aid,
I knew something was different
about this particular birth.
I walked into my mother's rooms
and found all my aunts
and even some of my cousins there.

When the first child of three
we pulled from her womb
was a girl, something
deep within my bones
understood that everything
was about to change.

A Shift

I noticed it first in my aunts.
How they looked at me strangely.
No one ever knows that they're different
until someone makes them feel it.

With the birth of each of my sisters,
vivid-eyed and bronze-skinned
like my mother and aunts,
I sensed how disparate I was.

Even my sisters born with tails or wings
wore them so prettily that my aunts spoke
of their soft beauty, a compliment
that was never paid to me.

As my many sisters grew, I found myself
more alone than ever.
They were born in schools,
inseparable from one another,

always on the riverbanks
together. I wished that I too
was born with another
who was regarded as serpentine like me.

When I looked in the mirror,
I saw a face I should love.
But instead, all I saw was
how unlike my family I was.

Equal, Unequal

Like me, my sisters,
the Oceanids,
were blessed with no gifts.

Unlike my sisters,
my father called upon me
for counsel.

When he claimed
he treated none of his children
differently from each other,

this was one place
where I did differ.
I would walk into his chambers,

that cerulean jewel,
made with walls of deep blue,
and he would ask me

about the nature of waves,
for my thoughts
on what he should build next,

or what Gaia needed
amongst her meadows
and fresh green forests.

'Styx,' he would say,
his stormy eyes observant
on the world before him,

'would this river work here?'
And I would shake my head
as I ruminated on it.

'It would flood easily,
and the forest is unfriendly
to a river running through it.

The mountains here, however,
would be a kinder place
to create a river.'

And with his hand he would
raise a world moulded with water,
a river through the mountains.

I would point out where
there were rivers and streams
needed and suggest

where land must end,
and where there should be
an ocean or a sea.

It filled me with pride to help him
this way. To be trusted by him
to help build his legacy.

Which is why it filled me
with an impotent rage
when he would then

hand over the guardianship of those rivers
and streams to one of my brothers
instead of giving even just one

to me.

The Day My Mother Stopped Giving Birth

was also the day all the Titans gathered
at our home. It was not strange
to see my aunts and uncles here.
Oceanus's halls were used to
the footfalls of divinity.

What did surprise me was
the way they were gathered
in the great hall.
And beyond that,
how *all* my many cousins were also there.

It was only when my grandmother
Gaia entered with her majestic siblings,
my great-aunt Nyx, the Night,
her consort Erebus, the Darkness,
and great-uncle Eros, of Love,

that I realized something peculiar
was happening. Why had all the Gods
collected in my father's halls?
I almost gasped when I saw
the ever-reclusive God-King

Kronos and his consort, Rhea,
in attendance. While the older Titans
and the Primordials sat in gold palatial chairs
by my father's polished aquamarine throne,
my cousins, brothers, and sisters

stood before them
keeping a respectful distance
from their powerful seats.

I took the opportunity
to look closely at my uncle

Kronos. His amber eyes
were wild, yet tired.
Beside him Rhea appeared pale.
By now we had all heard the story
of how Kronos had ripped

the first of Rhea's children
from her arms and devoured
the child whole. She had not
even had a chance to name the infant.
My heart twinged as I looked at her.

Once, her emerald eyes had sparkled
just like my mother's – her sister.
Now they were dulled
like the darkest sea glass,
a cold numbness in them.

I pulled my eyes away from her
as my father began to speak.
He too looked worn, as he sometimes
did when he spent too long
making a particularly complex waterfall.

'I know you are all surprised
to be summoned here.
However, our King,
my brother, has a declaration
that must be heard.'

My uncle, the God-King, rose,
nodding slightly at my father.
'It has been agreed
that Oceanus and Tethys
will have no more children.'

Gasps and whispers rung out
from my cousins and siblings
at this announcement.
It was unheard of that one Titan
told another what to do.

However, at his words,
I let out a sigh of relief.
I was no longer to be midwife
to my mother's many births.
But when I stole a glance
at my mother,

I saw her face was ashen,
there was bitter resentment
as she glared at Kronos.
I looked around the room
and understood sharply

what was happening.
My brothers and sisters and I
outnumbered our cousins
by a considerable amount.
The cold truth dawned on me.

We were a threat.
To a God-King who feared
being usurped by his own children,
the progeny of other Gods
were now also a concern.

But Kronos was not done.
'After a long discussion,
it has also been decided
that the Potamoi will be
River Gods, blessed

with full divine powers.
And the Oceanids
will live to serve and nurture
what was within their brothers'
rivers and their father's seas.'

None of my sisters reacted,
but I felt like my insides
had been crushed,
so much so that I forgot
both my place and my silence.

'But this means
we have *no* divine powers!
Nothing but our immortality!'
I felt the hard stare of my father
and heard the hiss of an angry aunt.

But my words were spoken
with such indignation
that Kronos's blazing eyes
found me
amongst all my siblings.

'Styx!'

It was the first time my mother
had even acknowledged me
in an age. The curse, I suppose,
of having thousands of children
is that you could spend an immortality
not speaking to some of them.

I did not turn to look at her.
Instead, I met the God-King's glare
with the hot, burning rage
I had carried within me for years.
My father's sea-blue halls
filled with tension.

I could feel
all my sisters behind me,
their fretting
only adding to my anger.
Of course, I would have to fight
for our futures all alone.

Kronos's next words boomed
across the silent hall,
a hidden violence in every word.
'Who is this insolent child
that dares to speak while
I am speaking!'

But I was not afraid of him.
I had lived a thankless lifetime
in the shadows whilst
my father handed the rivers
I had helped him make

to my brothers, and I had been
midwife to my mother.

I would not back away
and let myself be trampled
by an uncle I had only just met.
It was as though an uncontrollable rage,
one of never being seen,
spoke through me now.

I raised my head in his direction.
'I am Styx, the oldest child
of Oceanus and Tethys.
I was born at the start
of your reign, oh King,
the first of the Titan children.'

I could feel every eye in the room
turned in my direction.
The weight of my words
clearly had some impact.
Kronos's eyes narrowed
as he considered them.

Then imperiously he asked,
'And you think your position
is enough to challenge my decree?'
He turned to my father. 'Oceanus,
tell your child to leave my sight
before I punish her!'

I looked to my father, hopeful
that he would support me.
He knew my counsel well,
had always trusted me to advise
him. I knew my father would
stand by me when it mattered most.

It felt as though an era passed,
then my father rose slowly
from his chair to speak.
He opened his mouth
and spoke these words . . .

'Styx. Leave.'

At first, I thought I had misheard him.
This could not be the same father
whose rivers were built on my advice.

Not the God who stood by my side
on those golden sands reminding me
how deeply he and my mother cared for me.

But when I did not move,
his voice swelled with a storm.
'Styx. You *must* leave.'

'Not until someone tells me,'
I said with gritted teeth,
'what my sisters and I were made for.'

Kronos looked thunderous
but then a cruel smile formed at his lips.
'My dear child. Everyone needs

beautiful things to gaze at.
But I can see,' he added, looking
me up and down coldly,

'how this soft power eludes you.'
Titters rose behind me from the Oceanids,
foolish as they were not to realize

what they were being offered
was nothing. No power, no gifts.
Nothing to tie us to godhood

other than our lineage and immortality.
But what use is immortality
without any kind of power?

My rage tasted bitter on my tongue.
I opened my mouth to speak again,
only for my father's heavy voice to shout,

'ENOUGH. STYX.
I ASKED THAT YOU LEAVE.' My cheeks reddened
and I swallowed back tears of fury

as I shrivelled before his gaze,
turned and pushed past all my sisters,
running and running as far

as my feet could take me.

Racing

down the halls,
down past my father's chambers
where I helped him so much,
past my favourite hiding places
and my mother's birthing rooms,
past the grand ornaments and shells
placed so delicately around the palace.
And past the secrets and the laughs
I often heard at my own expense
from my sisters and my aunts.
I ran past the high arches
that felt so stifling now to me,
a reminder of father's decree,
of a home that felt hostile to me,
until I was outside.
Until I could not run
anymore, until I collapsed,
exhaustion clawing at me because
shame,
sadness,
anger
is not something
you can run from.

Out of Breath

I lay on the shores for a long time,
feeling the still-warm sand
under my heaving body.

Until I felt the tide,
cold and sweet against
my shame-warmed skin.

It wasn't so much
that I could not tolerate
the brutality of the dismissal.

But more that it was my father,
my sole ally, my protector,
who had betrayed me.

I should have known better
than to trust anyone
in this family.

After all, our greatest legacy
was a father butchered by his son
and exiled to a place no one knew.

Why was I expecting loyalty
from Oceanus, a God who still called Kronos
brother after what he had done to their father?

Not even just brother.
He honoured him as *king*.

When My Breath Returned,

slow and soft,
shallow and then deeper,
I raised myself from the wet sand,
lifted myself from the ocean's waves.

If I was a true Goddess,
I would not have run out
of my breath this fast,
my body would not weaken.

My fingers clenched
into fists as I stared at the sea,
thinking of how my sisters laughed at me
while I fought for their honour and mine.

Foolish girls cheering on
their own degradation, they did not see
how our brothers would get godhood
and untold power, and we were left with

nothing, but the hope
of good marriages while
we simply *preserved* what our brothers,
our parents, our aunts, uncles, and grandparents *made*.

Darkness Fell

My great-aunt Nyx raised her velvet cloak
and the sky was painted rich blue till it turned black.

The stars blinked at me and I thought of her:
Chaos, mother to us all, up there somewhere

still making the never-ending darkness beyond
vaster and vaster to accommodate her new creations.

Is this what she intended for her great-granddaughters?
That while there could be thousands of Gods,

thousands of Goddesses could not exist?
I wish I could speak to her. I closed my eyes.

And that was when I felt it.

A Strange Quiet Breeze

It couldn't have risen
from the azure calm of the ocean
and it could not have come
from a still-cooling sky.

And yet it persisted,
calm and gentle, till I looked around
to see where it was coming from.
I found it then, that hidden solace.

I rose from where I lay
in the wet sand and felt the breeze
on my face, dampening my anger.
My sharp eyes followed its trail.

I began to walk
in its direction. There, inside
the cliffs Gaia had crafted into the earth,
was an opening where seawater

flowed in freely. And it
was glowing.

The Sanctuary

It was a sea cave that went deep underwater, and like the rooms of a palace, revealed others opening into one another before the final cave opened onto wide waters. As I climbed the slippery moss-covered rocks, I made my way through the dark green seaweed, stepping into the fertile sand until I was finally at the mouth of this hidden treasure I had found. I thought it would be dark. But inside, the water glowed like it held pieces stolen from the sky. I watched in awe as these sky pieces glowed, and when I reached to touch one, it shimmered away from me. Gently, I cupped my hands and lifted one to examine it. I was surprised to discover that it was simply a small worm, but the glow it gave made it look more beautiful than a butterfly. Someone had blessed this ugly thing with such power, it could create beauty in the world. Gently putting it back into the water, I looked around this peculiar new place, a cavern made of grey rock and a deep pool at its centre. It seemed as though this sanctuary was untouched by anyone from my family, that even if some God or Goddess had made it, they had forgotten about it long ago. It was the first time in a long time that I had the complete unwatched, unstifled solitude I needed so desperately. Grateful, I closed my eyes and touched the pool gently, giving it a soft blessing. A tear rolled down my cheek to meet the waters and then . . .

Creation

It was as though my hand was gripped
by its very own force, and I felt it before
I could understand what it was.

An elongated, slimy body formed between
my fingers. In shock, I pulled my hand
from the water to stare at it,

and the creature twisted around my knuckles.
It had the markings of a leopard,
small black dots on its golden skin,

and its beady eyes looked into mine
as I lifted it to see its face. It had
small, sharp razor teeth and yet

it chose not to bite me.
I stared down at the waters of the cave.
Perhaps this was a place of creation,

the pool blessed by one of the Primordials.
But as the creature stared at me, I realized
it was waiting for my command.

That *I* was its maker. It needed me
to give it a purpose. I laughed bitterly.
What a strange irony, for me to tell

this animal what it was here for,
when I did not know my *own* purpose.
But this was a gift I could give my creature,

a gift no one had given me. I touched
its oily head and I said, 'You are an eel
and your gift is to live, just to be.'

I was about to place it in the water,
to allow it to swim away from me.
But before I did that, I had an idea.

Gently, I touched its tail and closed
my eyes as I had before,
touched the waters of the pool again,

until a spark of lightning rose
from the being's tail. I looked it in the eye.
'A gift of protection. From me to you.'

The thing did not speak to me,
but I sensed its thoughts, its needs. Slowly
I put it into the pool and let it swim free.

I Slept in the Cave That Night

I knew by now no one was coming to look for me.
If I listened carefully, I could hear the music,
the sound of divine feet dancing with my brothers
as my sisters played a myriad of songs.

The sound was faint compared to
the drip drip drip of the water from the cave
but somehow it still lulled me to sleep.
I dreamed of disquieting things: eels,

my father's thunderous face, and my brothers
and sisters laughing at my expense.
I tossed and turned on the hard rock floor
until finally my eyes snapped open.

And then I saw them.
A pair of feet
standing before me
close to where I slept.

Asteria

A CHILD MADE OF NEBULA AND PROPHECY

PART II

The Secret

The voices in my head
were whispering again,
they needed my guidance,
they wanted me to hear them,
they needed their prophecies—

'Asteria,' my mother spoke over them,
just before I left, 'remember
to return before Nyx flies
to paint the sky dark
so the stars can shine.'

I sighed. 'But, Mother,
are the stars not my realm?
Should I not stay to watch
them blinking and study
their glimmer and glow?'

My mother brushed
my dark curls away
from my face to look
into my violet eyes.
'Please, Asteria.

We are visitors in this palace,
and I would like you to spend
more time with your uncles
and aunts and cousins
while we are here.'

I would have pleaded more,
but I could see my younger sister,
Leto, watching me carefully.

Disobedience was not
a lesson I wanted to teach her.

So instead, I swallowed
my displeasure and nodded
at my mother. Before she could
ask more of me, I turned
and left our shared chambers

inside Oceanus's grand palace.
As I walked those gilded halls,
my nymph cousins called to me,
their riverbanks rich with flowers
as they sat laughing and sharing secrets.

But I simply waved to them
and kept going, quickening
my pace. Ever since we had arrived
for Kronos's grand decree,
I had been having dreams.

And the more dreams I had,
the more I needed to be alone.
I could not tell my mother,
or my father for that matter.
My parents were, after all,

the God of Intellect
and the Goddess of Prophecy.
They would make this larger
than I needed it to be,
or see it as a premonition

and I did not desire that yet.
I needed to know what it was
that I had seen and only
the water could tell me that.
So I made my way to

the one place I knew
I could be away from prying eyes
and be at peace. My own secret.
The little cave I had found an era ago,
which provided the solace I needed.

But when I jumped over
the craggy rocks covered in moss
to the familiar mouth
of my beloved sanctuary,
a cold surprise awaited me.

Someone
Was
Already
There
Asleep.

The Figure Awoke

and scrambled up.
In the low light of the cave,
I couldn't see much, but
I could tell they were tall.

As the being moved
farther into the light,
I saw it was her.
The daughter of Oceanus

who had crossed Kronos.
With her split eyes
and green hair, she was even
more fearsome in person.

I was a Goddess.
Fear was not a natural feeling
for our kind. But I felt its shudder
in my veins as I looked to her.

I did not show it. Instead
I pulled myself up to my full height,
still shorter than her, and spoke coldly.
'Why are you in my cave?'

'*Your* cave?' she said,
but it was not a question.
'This cave is near
my father's palace.

It belongs to my family.'
I blinked at this.
'No, it does not.
I have been visiting here

since I was a small child,
and I never saw you
or any of your family here
until today.'

She lifted her lips in a sneer
and showed me her fangs.
Instinctively, I took a step back,
recoiling in dread.

As She Stepped Forward

I stopped myself
from retreating any farther.

I had a right to be here.
My home, my father's palace,

was not far from this spot.
In fact, I had hidden one

of my biggest secrets here.
'If you do not believe me,'

I said quietly, 'look in
the water and see for yourself.'

Styx looked into the pool
and then turned back impatiently.

'There is nothing there.'
I scowled at her. 'Yes there is.

I created them myself,
those creatures that glow

and make the water shine like stars.
Look closer and—'

But as I turned to the pool,
I saw it. A dark, long serpentlike

thing that was devouring the last
of my prized creations.

I shrieked and Styx turned to see
what had horrified me.

To my fury and disgust,
she began to laugh.

My Rage Spoke Before I Did

and I launched myself at her
knocking us both to the ground
as she laughed at me.

How dare she.
How dare she.
HOW DARE SHE!

The anger in me was taking
the form of fists that landed
as blows on her face,

but like her anger and wit,
Styx was quick. She soon dodged
so my fists hit the ground

beside her instead, and then
her bony knees
grasped my hips and turned us over,

but before she could land
her fist in my face,
I grabbed her forearms

and tried to turn us over yet again.
This time, however,
we slipped over the edge

and into the water we fell.

Shock

I had never been fully immersed
in any water, either of this cave
or in the oceans and rivers outside.

So when we fell in,
I immediately started to struggle.
My legs lashed out at nothingness,

and when I felt it,
the smooth, slimy feel
of Styx's creature,

my heart thudded, and in my fear,
I kicked out at it,
only to find my foot met

a crevice in the cave's
underwater wall,
and as I tried to pull

and pull, my foot
would not free itself.
I was trapped underwater,

unable to get out.

Fear

I had never known it
until this day.

Never felt the way
it could wrap around

your very bones
like a serpent holding

its prey, just before
it sinks its fangs

deep into its neck.

The voices in my head,
usually whispers,

began to scream.
My heart felt like

it would burst
from my chest

as I thrashed about.
It was true,

I could not die,
but imagine an eternity

imprisoned undersea
in this dark cave,

never to see the night sky
or stars ever again.

A Hand Touched My Shoulder

and I turned to see Styx.
Her bright yellow eyes met mine
as she floated easily beside me.

Of course,
as one of Oceanus's children,
the water was her closest friend.

As she swam down to the crevice,
I felt my panic subside.
At least I was not alone here.

Styx pushed and pulled
at the rocks until finally
my foot was free.

My movements panicked as
I thrashed in my hurry to
escape from this near-prison

and broke through the water's surface,
grasping the rock wall
as I gulped in a deep breath of air.

Behind me I heard Styx rise too.
And as I hauled myself up
onto the rock, I watched her

swim over to me, the strange,
slimy, serpentlike creature
swimming circles

around her.
It was as though lightning
was escaping out of its tail,

but this did not bother Styx.
I reached out toward her,
offering my hand.

I thought she would refuse.
I think she wanted to.
But then

she took my hand
so I could hoist her
onto the rock next to me.

For some time,
neither of us spoke,
catching our breath.

The voices in my head
had soothed to a chatter
that brought me comfort.

My heart still thudding hard,
I turned to her
and said two gentle words.

'Thank You'

Styx did not reply. She simply sat there,
her dress sodden and her green hair damp,

until finally she began to chuckle.
I stared at her as she threw back her head,

eyes closed as her shoulders shook,
the whole cave filled with peals of laughter.

Her mirth was infectious,
because I too began to laugh

and soon the cavern resonated with
the sound, the freest of moments

that I had had in years. When we stopped,
our eyes filled with gleeful tears,

I said to Styx, 'The cave is yours.
You can keep it. With my gratitude.'

But to my surprise, she shook her head.
'You found it first. It is yours by right.'

The voices in my head whispered again
and their suggestion gave me pause.

I tilted my head as I looked around the cave.
'Perhaps there is another way.'

She nodded, reading my thoughts.
'Perhaps we should share it.'

An Interruption

'Asteria!' I heard a voice call.
I turned around and saw her,
my little sister, Leto.

Standing at the cavern's mouth,
her silhouette
was taller than I remembered it.

And I had just seen her this morning.
All Gods grow quickly,
but Leto was growing faster than most.

She was already nearly my height.
Her lovely heart-shaped face
was softened by the sun

and her golden eyes were bright.
I looked up at her and asked,

'What is it?'

'Mother wants you to attend the feast!'
I scowled at this. I did not want
to join the feast. I did not like

the attentions of the River Gods,
nor the prattle of my aunts.
I wanted to stay here.

Leto, seeing my face,
grimaced and said,
'You promised her you would.'

I sighed and stood slowly,
my eyes meeting Styx's.
'Would you like to join us?'

But this time she decisively
shook her head. 'I need time alone.'
I nodded and walked to my sister.

As we left, Styx called out,

'Asteria.' I turned to her.
'We can meet here tomorrow.'

And in those words,
I recognized the promise
of a new friend.

A Friendship Grew

When I had found this sanctuary, years ago, I never thought it would also become the place where I found my first ally. The palace of my father, Coeus the God of Intellect, was not far from here, which meant that the cave fell precisely halfway between Oceanus's palace and the house of Coeus, and so, Styx and I began to meet regularly inside this secret place we had decided to share. Styx asked me what it was like to be a Goddess and I led her outside to show her the stars that I could melt at my command. I asked her about her water gifts, and she told me because she was the eldest child of two of the old Titans and despite her father never blessing her, there were some powers that were innate to who she was as a water deity. She had taught herself how to bend water to her will, how to raise a small cyclone if she wished, and how every river and stream had been built by her father with her advice. But with Kronos's decree, Oceanus had stopped asking for her help and she could feel her few self-taught powers slipping away. I understood. For after Kronos's words, I had watched how the River Gods seemed much more powerful compared to their nymph sisters, who were now relegated to menial tasks like maintaining the life within their rivers and making the riverbanks prettier. The best they could hope for was a good marriage or to serve a Goddess. I could not imagine Styx doing either. There was a quiet power inside her, like a precious amber stone hiding within, a secret that no one else could see. And yet, every time she was with me, I felt it reverberate.

I Had a Secret Too

At my birth, my father had made me
Goddess of Oracles and Falling Stars.
With this gift also came the voices in my head.

Gods do not work with time in linearity.
We do not have death to march toward.
These voices were from Oracles scattered across time.

They told me stories about who they were.
That they had prophecies about posterity.
That they needed me to guide them.

When I was a child, I spoke to the voices
openly, until my mother pulled me aside
and told me to speak to them in my mind.

Not long after, once when Hyperion
set the sun and I watched it
gleam burnt marigold across

the turquoise ocean, I heard a call.
Asteria. I rose from my bed.
Asteria. I followed it

to the white sand outside my room.
Asteria. And as Nyx painted the sky and Selene,
the Moon Goddess, danced across the dark,

I saw it. The star that called
my name. It was bright red
like a ruby. When I reached out

and plucked it from the sky,
it spoke. 'Plant me amongst
the violets and watch me grow.'

I did as I was told,
half thinking I was in a dream.
The next day amongst the violets

a cascade of ruby-red flowers
with a swirl of petals like
a fine silk dress grew.

I do not know what force
called to me
from the darkness to find the star.

To treat it like a seed to be planted,
to be nourished by my hands
so it would flower.

Something deep within
told me that I should not
speak of this to anyone.

That no one
should ever know
what I had done.

Shared Secrets

'Where are we going?'
Styx asked again,
as I led her from the cave,
with its safe mossy rocks.

I turned to her.
'You will see, I promise.'
Styx grumbled to herself,
'Just because you're the Goddess

of Oracles doesn't mean
everything has to be a secret.'
I laughed at her words
and shot back,

'Patience! Have I lied to you yet
or led you astray?'
Styx retorted, 'There is
a first time for everything.'

I stopped suddenly when I saw it,
the way the golden sands in front of
Styx's home finally gave way
to white sands in front of mine,

the sun catching the crimson flowers
and the violet beyond,
my most precious secret.
I took Styx's hand.

'We are here,' I said.

Styx Picked One of the Red Flowers

and looked at it carefully.
Then she turned to me and asked,
'I assume that these are your creations?
What called to you to create them?'

I nodded. 'It was almost like
the prophecy voices I hear,
but different. It felt like a dream
but it was not, it was . . .'

But Styx was already walking
toward the violet flowers
beyond my crimson creations.
She paused there for a long time.

Her face was torn between
wonder and thoughtfulness.
'Do you remember
what happened to Ouranos?'

'Of course,' I said. 'After Kronos
cut off his manhood, his blood sprang free
and where it landed, it gave us the giants,
and the Furies, and ash-tree nymphs.'

Styx gazed down at the violets.
'And these have been here for
as long as you know?'
I picked through her trail

of thoughts and realized
what she was suggesting.

'You think that these violets
are born from divine blood?'

She had a faraway look
in her eyes now as she stared
from the violets to the sea.
'I think ichor has done

stranger things than this.'
Then she turned to me.
'And I think you were right
to keep this strange garden a secret.'

She did not ask the question
of what my crimson flowers were for.
And yet it told me that no one else
but Styx and I should know

that I made them.

Styx's Voice Held a Mystery

When I looked into her split eyes I saw
a thousand stories unfold in a moment.

There was warning and peril,
but it was encased with ambition and wonder.

'Styx,' I whispered softly, my voice
carried by the breeze.

'Do you remember
when you made the eel?'

Her mouth set in a thin line as she said,
'I think that was a mistake.'

I shook my head. 'It was not.
You and I, we can do things

that *they* have not blessed us with.'
Styx looked down

at the crimson flower in her hand.
'If we can make things like this.

Things that did not exist before—'
I took her hand and finished for her.

'What else can we do
that they do not think we can.'

Exploration

We returned to our cave
with the crimson and violet flowers.

Styx dropped the violet flowers in the water
and we waited to see if anything happened.

We waited for them
to reveal some kind of magic property,

to show us some kind of dreamlike quality.
But when they just floated in the water,

the eel swimming around them
with curiosity, I had a thought.

'What if . . . what if we are wrong about it
being Ouranos's blood that made the violets.'

Styx stared at me thoughtfully,
her expression laced with questions.

'What are you suggesting?'
I watched the sleek black eel

swimming in the water.
Then I looked into Styx's eyes.

'I am saying,' I said softly,
'try to make the eel again.'

Practice

But it was not so simple.
Styx's first attempt ended
with nothing in her hands.

Her second caused her to leave
half-moon marks on her own palms
from clenching them too hard.

On the third attempt,
Styx looked annoyed, upset,
and like she was about to give up.

I would not let her.
We were sitting on the rocks,
and Styx was concentrating,

trying to remember how
she had magicked the eel.
'It is no use,' she said finally,

opening her eyes after another try.
'How were you feeling that day?'
I asked her. 'The day I found you

sleeping inside the cave?'
This made her bare her fangs.
'I would rather not speak about it.'

I rubbed my forehead. 'I think you
need to bring back that pain.
I think your anger helped you that day.'

Styx closed her eyes again and tried
with all of her might to remember.
Her face was a mask of concentration

and as her hand touched the water,
I saw it. Something was forming
between her hand and the water.

At first, I thought it was another eel.
But instead, this creature was small.
A tiny red shell formed,

and then two large angry pincers.
Two beady little eyes
and many, many legs.

Styx held the thing up in wonder
as it moved its pincers this way and that.
I stared at it in fascination.

'What were you thinking about
when you made that?' I asked.
She looked up at me as she set

her creation onto the rock.
It moved sideways quickly
until it was hidden in a crevice.

'I was thinking,' she said,
looking at me with a wry smile,
'how infuriating all of this is.'

I let out a surprised laugh
and Styx's smile widened.
She reached down and picked up

a small stone in her fingers.
I touched her hand gently,
holding the flower against it.

And that was how
the first starfish was born.
A creature Styx and I made together.

Reasons for Secrets

I had been raised not to keep them.
In the house of the God of Intellect,
there was no point in keeping secrets.

He and my mother would find out,
or Leto would draw them out of me.
But when my Oracles in my mind

chattered too loud and my mother
had taught me how to hide them,
I understood that my gifts were not

always understood nor welcome.
A gift of prophecy always made
Gods without such talents wary of me.

I could see what even the God-King
could not see, into posterity.
And so any new gifts I found,

like my gift of crimson flowers,
I knew well to hide them.
There was only so many unusual powers

Goddesses could hold
before the Gods put restrictions on us
the way Kronos had on Styx

and her sisters.

More Practice

While we had learned
more about Styx's powers,
that they were influenced
by her feelings – the dark eel
was born from her rage,
the red crab as we called it
was born from her annoyance –

we still didn't know
where my abilities of creation
came from. I knew somehow
they were linked to
my prophetic dreams and how
I could pluck stars from the sky.
But knew neither how nor why.

We sat on the golden beach
watching Nyx paint the sky black,
her chariot infusing ink-dark smoke
into the blue of the day,
turning it into the night.
'Have you tried making something
without waiting for a dream or a calling?'

Styx asked me this question
as the stars came out slowly,
blinking in our direction.
I shook my head. 'No.
Even the glowworms
were born from the innermost
heart of a dying star.'

Styx was quiet a moment,
then picked up a piece of sea glass
at my feet. 'How do you know,'
she asked, handing it to me,
'whether you can create without
the use of stars or dreams
if you do not try?'

Sea Glass and Spellwork

Styx and I collected all the sea glass
we could find on the shoreline
between our fathers' palaces.

We arranged our colourful glass –
turquoise, amber, emerald, ruby –
in a circle, and I tried the same trick

that Styx did. I attempted to use
my feelings to transform
the sea glass into other things.

I closed my eyes and imagined
the emerald sea glass in my hand
was a sapling, a leaf, something

living. Something breathing.
When nothing happened,
I lifted a ruby sea glass

and tried to envision
my crimson flowers.
Again nothing happened.

'It took me time too,'
Styx said with quiet encouragement.
'Perhaps we should try it another way.'

I nodded reluctantly,
sighing in disappointment.
'Perhaps I must use something living.'

I went into the cave and picked
up the flowers we had brought back with us.
I lifted one crimson bloom

and studied it carefully,
then ran back with it to Styx.
She handed me the ruby sea glass.

I closed my eyes and murmured softly
that the piece of sea glass
was now a scarlet flower.

A strange sensation filled
both my hands. Warm and kind,
full of awe and wonder.

I opened my eyes and looked down
At the piece of glass in my hands.
Except it was no longer sea glass.

My cupped hands held crimson flowers.
Styx clapped her hands in delight,
the happiest I had ever seen her.

'Asteria,' she breathed,
'look at what you can do.
You took a piece of sea glass

and made it into something living.'
And whilst this was small
compared to Styx's creations,

the fact that I had managed to create
without waiting for permission
from a dream or a calling

felt like powerful in a way
I had never felt before.
And the voices in my head sang.

As Well as Triumphs, There Were Mistakes Too

Like the moment Styx
accidentally created
three poisonous sea snakes

and we had to spend a morning
fishing them out of the cave pool
and releasing them into the ocean.

She must have been
particularly upset
with her siblings that day.

Or my accident where
I transformed my own hand
into amber sea glass

and it took Styx and I
all day to change it back.
For days after,

whenever I tried to use that hand,
it felt like I was moving a heavy stone.
Or when Styx, in her rage at her brothers,

created more eels
and we were stung repeatedly
by them as we tried to release

them all into the sea.
And the time I nearly destroyed a comet
by planting it into the ground,

not realizing it was new and hungry
and it would fight to be in the sky again.
It made us both fly into the sea

as it fought its way out
and raised itself into the night above.
We accepted quickly

that all of these were lessons.
Gifts took patience to learn,
to understand, and all these mistakes

were simply a way of knowing
how our newfound powers worked
and how they did not.

Danger Beyond

As much as I tried to ignore it
I could feel Styx's unhappiness every day.

I knew that being with me was an escape
from her father's palace.

Even as we practised these secret gifts,
it was hard to ignore what Oceanus's palace meant.

Styx could not have a moment of peace
for it felt like her family was always watching her.

Once in a less reserved moment, Styx said,
'The walls are prisons with eyes.'

I could not imagine how that felt.
And with Kronos's decree hanging over them,

I knew that our days spent together
in practice meant more to Styx than learning.

This was the only place she could breathe free.

A Change In Hierarchy

It happened slowly.
As the River Gods grew in power
and the Oceanids diminished in theirs,

a secondary hierarchy
began to form
amongst the nymphs.

I noticed it when I visited Oceanus's palace
with my parents.
The first thing my cousins did

was grasp my arms
and lead me away.
I looked for Styx amongst

these pearly skinned,
gossamer-dressed nymphs,
each one with glossy silken hair

and eyes that shone
sapphire, ruby, or emerald,
but her amber split eyes were missing.

'Come, cousin,' said Acaste,
her waist-length lustrous brown hair
woven with soft grey flowers.

'You must sit with us
at the favoured seat by
our mother's throne.'

As she said this,
she pushed aside
the weeping willow leaves

that obscured the view
of Goddess Tethys's freshwater lake.
The turquoise-and-azure water

shimmered invitingly, as
all along the edges
laughing nymphs played

with dolphins
and tended to silver fish.
In the centre of it all,

was a gleaming throne
made from countless pearls
for Tethys herself,

though at this moment,
the throne was empty,
its beauty incomplete.

Acaste and her sisters
led me there on the backs
of large sea turtles.

I thanked my sea turtle
with a gentle pat on the head
and sat uneasily on

a rock covered with soft moss
while the nymphs asked me
dozens of questions.

'What is it like to own the stars?'
asked rosy-lipped Amphiro,
taking a fine seashell comb

to my long, untameable hair.
'I don't own the stars,' I told
the gaggle of waiting nymphs.

'I only help them fall
when they need to.'
Acaste scoffed at my words.

'Callirhoe said you could melt
the stars at your whim.
That means they are yours!'

I sighed, trying to find the words
to explain that the caretaking of stars
was a responsibility, not ownership,

but just then Styx emerged
from the waters of the lake,
long green hair dripping.

'Styx.' Acaste frowned at her.
'I thought we told you this before
that you are to stay away.'

Styx gave her a smile designed
to infuriate. 'Did you? I don't recall.
Your voice is so soft, Acaste.'

Acaste's frown darkened to
a scowl and the other nymphs
murmured and whispered.

'This is not your place, Styx.
Mother has chosen her favourites.
You are not amongst them.'

I let out a gasp at this cruelty
and Styx's eyes met mine,
with a slight shake of her head.

Her smile grew nastier.
'I may not be one of mother's
trinkets of the moment,

but I will always be
the first of all of us.
My position is untouchable.'

Her other sisters let out
horrified huffs at this,
but I felt a gleam of pride.

'Your position once mattered,'
Acaste said, tossing her hair
behind her perfect shoulder,

but that was before.
It is *us* who are favoured now,
by the Gods and their brothers.

Only beauty counts. And you,'
she said pityingly,
'are not beautiful.

What match
can you hope
to make?'

Styx's eyes flashed with fury
as she glared at Acaste
and I stepped off the rock

away from the grasp
of all these nymphs
and their cruelty and smother.

'Do not speak to her like that.'
I glowered. 'NEVER speak
to your older sister that way.'

The skies above us darkened
as I dimmed the stars and went to Styx.
The nymphs shrank back from us.

I took her hand in the water.
'One day, Acaste,' Styx said,
a tremor of rage in her voice,

'you will realize the disservice
you have done yourself
by defining yourself by your beauty

and nothing more to speak of.'
With these words spoken,
we swam back through the lake

away from the gossiping tongues
and the cruel beauty that would be
the unmaking of Styx's sisters.

I Disliked Swimming

I had hated it even more since
I had been trapped in the pool
and Styx saved me.

But I would swim
a thousand lakes and seas
for Styx that day.

When we reached
the other side,
we walked through

the curtain made of
willow tree leaves.
I looped her arm in mine

as we made our way
through the high arches
of Oceanus's marble halls.

She did not speak,
but her silence
made me realize

how much she was
used to carrying
alone.

I only had one sister,
Leto. And I could not recall her
ever being this cruel to me.

Styx saw me
looking at her
and then looked away.

'Don't, Asteria,'
she said quietly.
I frowned at this.

We both stopped walking,
my gown still wet
from our unwanted swim.

'Don't look at me
with such pity.'
She turned to me.

'I do not need pity.'
Her voice vibrated
with ambition and spite . . .

'I Need Power'

I tensed at her words
as a pair of River Gods
walked by, their weathered
features deep in discussion.

Quickly, I grabbed
Styx's hand and pulled
her into a corner where the arch
hid us from the hallway.

'Styx,' I said quietly,
'keep your voice down!'
She pulled her hand
roughly out of mine.

'Why?' she asked bitterly.
'I do not want this version
of immortality. Where I am
judged for how I look,

not what I can do.
Where nymphs like Acaste
treat me with such disdain
while my parents silently watch

and even *you* look at me
with such pity in your eyes!'
I stared at her, my mouth open
at this outburst.

Had I not just defended her
in front of her sisters?
Had she not seen how much
I was willing to do for her?

As though she could
read my mind,
Styx pulled back from me
and said coldly,

'You are not here all the time.
And I do not need protection
when *I* can create life, and
NONE of them can.'

Her breathing was becoming
ragged now and to my shock
I realized Styx,
brave Styx,

was about to burst into tears.
I moved forward cautiously
and took her hand again.
She was in pain.

How could I help her?
'Styx, I beg you—'
That was when we heard
the footsteps and the words

'Kronos's Reign Is Not Secure'

It was my father's voice.
And he was saying the most dangerous
of things I had ever heard him say.

Why would he ever speak these words?
I looked at Styx and she met my gaze
with the same determination.

We let the footsteps leave
us and then followed them
at a safe, silent distance.

I could see Oceanus's
long, flowing white hair
and my own father's shiny

dark curls as their heads
were bent close together
deep in conversation

while they walked.
Styx said softly,
'There is a place to listen.

Come with me.'
Any hesitation I had
was overtaken by curiosity.

I nodded, taking her arm,
and we waited for them
to enter Oceanus's chambers.

Then Styx pulled at my elbow
and led me into a hidden alcove.
There was barely enough room

for the both of us, but suddenly
we heard Oceanus say,
'I had disagreed before.

But now, after this fourth child
and the news from Rhea
of his descent into madness,

I am inclined to agree.'
My father's voice had
a note of craftiness to it.

A tone I heard him often use
when he was convincing
others of his own ideas.

'Rightfully, as the eldest,
you should lead us.
You have the most children.

So many that Kronos
had to issue a decree
against you.'

Oceanus's voice was cautious,
'I have no interest in ruling,
you know this, Coeus.

My home,
my children,
my realm, is enough for me.'

My father's voice dropped
slightly. 'But look how
he treated you in your own

realm, Oceanus.
He has grown too
arrogant, he forgets his place.'

Styx's eyes widened
at these words.
I almost gasped.

'He is God-King.
That is his place,
you know this well.'

Oceanus's voice held
annoyance in it
and a warning.

But my father was growing
more impatient
and argumentative.

'Ask me why I only
have two daughters.
Do you think I do not want more?

Do you think I do not want a son?'
My eyes narrowed at this.
He had never expressed

any such sentiment.
Oceanus was silent
as my father continued.

'I do not feel
Kronos's rule is stable enough
to bring more Titan children

into this world.'
Both Styx and I clapped
our hands over our mouths.

The noise must have travelled
because the two Gods went silent.
For a terrible moment, all was still.

And then Oceanus's voice boomed,
'Who stands behind my door?'
Styx and I took this as our sign

to run.

We Did Not Stop Running Until We Reached Our Cave

My mind raced with questions
and my breath quickened
as my feet ran across
cool marble floors then to warm sand.

When we were finally there,
safe in our hallowed cavern,
with its welcoming water
and the azure glow of my worms,

we crumpled to the floor.
Quietly, with just the sound
of our own heavy breath,
we sat in contemplation.

'Do you think,' Styx asked,
'if my father becomes king,
there is a chance for my sisters
and I to be more than nymphs?'

I considered her question.
'I think,' I said softly, remembering
what Coeus said about desiring
a son, 'that even if our fathers

were rulers, every Goddess or nymph
would always be beholden to someone.'
Styx contemplated this,
her split eyes pensive.

'Surely . . .' she said eventually,
'all Gods cannot be so cruel.
Some of them must know
the kindness of mercy.'

A few minutes passed by
and then we heard the sound
of footsteps.
We looked at each other,

fear caught inside our eyes.
Was it our fathers?
Had we been seen?
What would the punishment be

for listening to what we should
never have heard.

Styx

SECRETS AND SALUTATIONS

PART III

A Silhouette Shadowed the Cave's Mouth

and as it came closer,
Asteria and I heaved a sigh of relief.

It was only Leto, my friend's younger sister.
Asteria reached her hand out

to welcome her into the cavern.
Usually, I would glower,

as the cave belonged to just Asteria and me,
but Leto's expression gave us both pause.

'Leto?' Asteria asked with concern,
looking into her sister's terrified eyes.

'You must come with me *now.*'
Her tone was urgent, and for a moment,

I thought she was just talking to Asteria.
Instead, she was looking at us both.

'It's your mother, Styx.
Something is wrong.'

I stood up slowly, not letting
my confusion show.

'Why would she send you?'
I asked, my question a blunt arrow.

'I have myriad sisters
she could send.'

Asteria shot me a warning look,
her arm around her sister.

I kept my gaze strong on Leto
as she hesitated to speak.

'We Are All to Go to Her Chambers'

Leto's words added to my confusion.
I stared at her. 'Asteria and you as well?'
I asked, deeply perplexed.

The only times Tethys ever asked me
to come to her chambers was during childbirth.
But she was not pregnant.

Something was wrong.
I felt Leto's words before my mind
could catch up with their implication.

I gave a terse nod to Leto,
and looked at Asteria. 'We will go.'
Sensing the urgency in my tone,

Asteria rose and grabbed Leto's hand.
They followed me as I ran back
to the palace, my heart pounding

as loudly as my feet.

Tethys's Chambers

I knew how much my father
loved my mother the first time I saw
the chambers he had built for her
above his great winding river.

When she told him the prophecy
of all the children she would bear,
he gathered the pearls of every oyster,
plucked sapphires from the seafloor,

and found the brightest marble from
as far as he could go into the earth's core.
He returned and built her this part
of the palace, every room made

of rich marble, carefully carved
windows spilled light everywhere
inside, and the sapphires and pearls
reflected the glow of the sun

into her chambers. My father knew
that to be wedded to him was also
to be wedded to his spending his time
underground as this was where his river ran.

So he built my mother the opposite,
a place of sunshine and warmth
where she could birth their many children
in a peaceful place full of light and breeze.

But today as I ran into these chambers,
I saw only the storm gathered above.
Darkness shadowed the room,
the sapphires looked onyx,

and even the pearls a threatening grey.
My mother was lying in her bed
and to my surprise, Asteria's mother, Phoebe,
was there, holding a cloth to her forehead.

When Phoebe moved,
my eyes widened as I saw why.
It was only us in this room.
My mother's womb was swollen

with a child she had sworn
to Kronos that she would not have.

'Styx, Come Here!'

My aunt Phoebe spoke with urgency.
My body did as it was told, even in shock.
I knew how to help my mother through this,
having helped with all my siblings' births.

I grabbed the clean water, and rushed
to be by my mother's side.
Phoebe told Asteria and Leto,
'Asteria, we need you here too.

Leto, go and make sure no one
disturbs us. Not a single soul
must be allowed in, do you understand?'
Leto nodded quickly and rushed

to stand outside the doors of the chambers.
As my mother let out a cry,
Phoebe gently took her hand.
'Hush, sister. I know this is difficult,

but we need your quiet now.'
To my surprise, proud Tethys obeyed,
taking a cloth, placing it in her mouth,
and biting down on it instead of screaming.

As Asteria and I helped,
Phoebe gently guided my mother
through the painful process
of bringing new immortal life

into this world. The labour was long,
much longer than any of the others
I had tended to.
Finally, a head emerged,

and then, like the strange miracle
she was, the child slid into my arms.
I waited to see if there was another.
But no, like me, she was alone.

I Placed Her on My Mother's Chest

as I had done with all my sisters before.
But instead of pulling her close
and blessing her, my mother simply
turned her head away.

'Styx,' Phoebe said, taking the baby
from my mother's chest,
'you are to tell no one of this.'
She looked to Asteria too.

'Either of you.' She swaddled
my new sister in silken threads,
and held her close. 'I will tell the world
that she is mine. And she will live

in Coeus's and my palace.'
I stared at the baby, unable
to understand what was happening.
'But she is my sister.'

My voice was small and hoarse.
'She is.' Phoebe paused, then said
kindly, placing her hand
on my face, 'You should name her.'

I touched my baby sister's head.
My heart ached to know her already.
'Metis. Call her Metis,' I whispered.
Phoebe nodded, and before I could

wish her well, spirited the child out the door,
walking quickly from Oceanus's palace.
I heard a soft whimper and I turned.
There, my majestic mother

was already on her feet as she was
after every single birth.
But this time, her eyes were filled
with a thousand unshed glistening tears.

I felt a hand take mine and squeeze,
and turned to look at Asteria's face.
All I saw there was kindness and sorrow.
And for the first time I gave myself

permission to let someone hold me as I wept.

A Reckoning

I had thought I understood how little
to expect from my mother and father.
I thought I had learned by now
what it meant
to live in the shadows.

But the way my mother had turned
away from Metis. The way she
had chosen not to *see* her
taught me something new.
There was an even darker quality

to this world of Titans.
A hierarchy where even a child
of Gods must abide by the rules,
accept being sent away in secret,
unclaimed by those who should

celebrate who you are at your birth.

Asteria's Embrace Was Kind

Her words were gentle. 'We will care for her
as our own sister. Do not worry yourself.'

But I was full of concern for my infant sister.
While I knew she would be safe with Asteria and Leto,

it did not change the fact that she was born
against the orders of a God-King,

putting her immortality in imminent danger.
Pulling myself from Asteria's embrace,

my eyes red with crying, I turned to my mother,
now sitting on her bed, already healed.

'How could you risk this?'
I hissed, rage starting to simmer.

My mother did not answer,
so I dug my claws deeper.

'You knew what would happen.
And now Metis must pay the price.'

My mother turned to me and for a second
I thought I saw sadness in her eyes

before it turned to anger.
'You may be favoured by your father,

and allowed to speak this way to him.
But you have no right to disrespect me so.'

I let go of Asteria's hand, my fury at its peak.
'I have every right as the deliverer of EACH

of your countless children! I have every right
as the oldest of your children to ask why

you would do this to your own daughter – my sister!'
My mother stared at me for a moment,

then spoke with a sadness I couldn't define.
'I hope one day you do not have to make

the choice I have made for her, daughter.
I hope your children are born into a safer world.'

I turned away in anger and left the room
before I said something darker,

sickened and afraid all at once.
If my mother, a Goddess, could not

give birth with safety, what hope
was there for one such as me?

Asteria Followed Me

Her hands grasped my shoulders
before I could leave the gilded halls,
the oppressive archways of my father's palace.

I stopped and turned to her,
meeting her eyes with my own
wrathful, fearful ones.

'How could she do this?'
I asked her furiously.
'Why would she give her away?'

Asteria sighed and rubbed her forehead.
'Do you not see why? Truly?
How else could your mother

keep you and all your siblings safe?'
Somewhere within me a voice of reason
understood Asteria's words.

But my own pain was too raw.
'What does it matter?' I said bitterly.
'My mother is used to throwing

daughters away. She has so many.'
Asteria quietly took my hand.
'I know you are in pain,'

she whispered kindly,
'but I promise I will care
for your sister as my very own.'

When I did not answer she added,
'Consider this. She will grow up
as one of three instead of one

of three thousand.'
At these words, my heart leaped,
a piece of hope lodging

in my bones.
After a moment I said,
'When she is old enough,

will you bring her to the cave?'
Asteria nodded immediately
'If no other of her birth family,

she will at least know you, Styx.
The best of you all.' My eyes filled again
but I held my tears back.

Instead, I squeezed Asteria's hand.
A gentle gesture that she would know
is my only way of saying

Thank you.

A Divine Child Grows

The birth of a divine child is always a holy event, but the growth after is witnessed by only a few. Unlike mortals, we grew at a cosmic pace. Metis was no different. Within days of her birth, Asteria brought her to our cave. She was small, but walking by herself, able to form full sentences. Her white hair fell in waves down her back and her yellow eyes reminded me so much of my own as a child. The difference was that hers were not split eyes like my serpent ones. Instead, they were golden, different from all of our nymph sisters. I knew Metis was special from the moment she walked into our cave and, self-assured, dove gracefully into the water to swim with the eel. When she was done, she reached a hand out to mine for help, and wordlessly, I pulled her up onto the rocky surface. Asteria had brought Leto, whom I would normally treat with the same distrust as my own sisters, but when I saw how she held Metis, her hands brushing her wet hair aside and kissing her brow, my heart softened. Metis in turn bestowed warm embraces upon us and reacted with wonder toward all we showed her. It was here in the cave that I learned what Metis was. How much more important it was that she was kept hidden from Kronos and his decrees. How alike she and I actually were. And how deeply afraid I was that she would one day disappear as quickly as she had appeared.

Metis

was a law unto her own.
She was a study in quickness.
As she grew from child to girlhood,
she also grew a hunger for knowledge.

There was something else
I discovered in those early years
of Metis's life. Things I wish
I had not ignored.

Once, I thought I saw sparks
escape the ends of her fingertips
to light the fire we had built
on a colder day out at the sea together.

A fleeting thought had passed then,
that Metis was also strange,
different as Asteria and I
had always been.

And as Asteria and I learned
more about our secret abilities,
our capacities to create,
more than once,

I felt the warm glow of her
amber eyes, watching us make magic
when we thought she was not there
from inside the cave, inside the dark.

Even in that era, when I realized
Metis was an unstoppable force,
what would happen if she learned
the truth of who she really was.

Years from Now
I Will Lie About This Story

When Asteria's lonely daughter
asks me about her mother,
I will pretend that I did not know
how she created the fox.

But the truth is I was there.
I walked with her into the woods
that day. I followed Asteria and
I watched her pluck a dying star

from the night sky. I watched her hold
the fiery thing in her bare hands.
I found her the bones of that long-dead
creature she asked me for.

I saw the way she tenderly placed
the beating heart and lungs of the star
inside that perfectly preserved dead thing.
I took her hand while we waited.

And that fox made of fire and stars
came to life and blinked before us.
Long tail leaving sparks everywhere
as it swished and moved.

When we walked out of the woods together,
the fox at our heels, Leto spied on us and asked
how we had done it. And we swore her
to the same secrecy we had sworn each other.

No one could ever know.

Sisters

I had always been mistrustful of sisters.
Perhaps it was because of my own.
I had only ever known sisters
to be constantly cruel to one another.

I had witnessed so many nymphs
treat each other kindly only to turn on one
another when it came to receiving attention.
I had forgotten that my sisters, like I, had to survive.

When Asteria first brought Leto to the cave,
I had felt an uncomfortable well of mistrust
within my belly when I saw her.
I know now that this was both fear and jealousy.

I waited for her to betray Asteria the way
my sisters betrayed one another.
But when I watched them together,
I noticed it. Asteria and Leto

were all they each had. And they did not
see each other as competition.
Instead they saw each other as soulmates.
Instead they saw each other as friends.

I did not have this with any of my sisters.
Perhaps I could have had this with Metis.
But she only knew me as cousin.
Nothing felt lonelier.

Change Came Suddenly

When you are immortal,
you learn to take life for granted.

The nights and the days
blend together into one

when you are not marching
in the direction of death.

So little prepares you for tumult
of any kind at all.

And so it was a day when Hyperion's
chariot was especially bright

in the sky, and Asteria and I sat
in the soft white sand, our toes just

touching the sea's waves
as they kissed the shoreline

before leaving again.
In the distance, we watched

as Metis and Leto played
with the little fox,

fire and sparks dancing
as they chased it across the beach.

I turned to Asteria and asked the question
that had troubled me since Metis's birth.

'Your father . . . does he know
that she is not his own?'

Asteria did not turn to look at me.
'If he does know, he has said nothing.

He blessed Metis as a Goddess though,
just like Leto and me.'

Although I knew this already,
I felt a bitterness on my tongue.

I knew this was envy, and quickly,
I swallowed it away.

Was it not better that Metis had
the power of goddesshood to protect her?

Instead I asked softly,
'What has he made her the Goddess of?'

She smiled at me and took my hand.
'You will be proud. She is the Goddess of—'

'Is this where you go to hide?'
A cruel, lilting voice interjected
before she could finish.

A Disturbance

When they asked me about my sisters,
I told Asteria and Leto I was close with none.
And while this was true, there were some
I hated more than others.

Acaste, with her cold emerald eyes,
and her cruel, beautiful followers,
Amphiro and Callirhoe, were
my least favourite of all.

Now here they were,
close to my and Asteria's sacred cave.
Standing on what I had known
as safe sands away from them.

They were a corruption of nymphs.
Their unkindness had many targets
and my loneliness, they had assumed,
had made me one too.

This mistake had cost them in the past.
It would cost them again.
I got to my feet, as did Asteria,
to look them in the eye.

'Why,' I hissed slowly, venomously,
'are you here?'

'We always wonder where you disappear
to, my dear sister.' Acaste's poisonous
smile was not lost on me.
'So we came out to find you.'

From the corner of my eye,
I saw Leto and Metis approach
with their new pet fox.
'Well, you have found me,' I said.

'Indeed, we have,' Acaste replied.
The air felt like it was touched with
a crackle of storms. The three of them
did not move even when Metis reached them.

'Perhaps it is time for you to go.'
Asteria addressed the nymphs.
She looked at me, then at Metis.
Acaste's gaze turned to her.

'Is this your new sister?' she smiled,
and Metis, still innocent to the world,
smiled back. 'Shame about her eyes.
Yellow eyes make her look like a snake.'

Acaste turned back to me. 'Just like you, Styx.'
My fists clenched as I saw Metis's face fall.
'Leave her be, Acaste. Or I will—'
A gentle hand touched my shoulder

and I whirled around to see Leto.
Leto stepped forward between us,
shielding Metis and me
from their cruel gaze.
'If you have something to say,'
Leto said quietly, 'say it.'
Amphiro sniffed in her direction.
'We would rather address Styx.'

Leto's next words were measured.
'And you are standing before three Goddesses.'
Asteria's voice joined her sister's.
'Remember your place. Speak or leave.'

At the invoking of divine superiority,
goddesshood over their nymph status,
my sisters backed down reluctantly
to my own satisfaction.

'Apologies,' Acaste murmured,
proud shoulders hunching slightly.
'You have all been summoned
to our father's halls.'

'Why?' Leto asked as Metis slipped
her little hand in hers. When they did not
answer, she spoke louder.
'I asked why.'

Her voice was as electric as my eel,
the threat of a thunder within it.
'They . . . The brothers are here,'
Callirhoe said quickly.

Asteria and I frowned at each other.
'What brothers?' I asked,
but my sisters were already backing away,
cowering from Leto's gaze.

I Turned to Leto

'Clearly,' I said quietly,
'I have underestimated you.'

Leto shook her head.
'You did not. I didn't think

I had it in me to do that.'
I tilted my head and examined her.

'That was one of the most impressive
displays of quiet power I have ever seen.'

Leto blushed and smiled shyly
as Metis and the fox jumped around her.

Asteria beamed and took my hand
then Leto's hand in her own.

'I knew you would
become friends one day.'

'I would not go that far,'
I said bluntly, but then I saw

Metis's little face turn to me
with big, worried eyes.

'But it's certainly a start,'
I conceded, and her smile returned.

A Feast

My father's palace was widely known
for its banquets, but this was grander
than any other feast he had ever held.
As we stepped past the marble pillars,
it felt like the gilded hall shone brighter
than ever before. Torches lit the corners
of every room and the pearl sheen
of the ceiling made it look bright and open.
One would almost forget parts of
this palace were underground.

I caught the arm of one of my brothers.
'Who is this feast in honour of?'
I asked him. He stared at me in confusion.
'Do you not know? Pallas and
Perses have come to stay with us.'
I frowned at this. The God of Weaponry
and his brother the God of Destruction?
'Why are they staying here?' I whispered.

He was an exceptionally irritating one
of the Potamoi, with big blue barnacles
that made up his beard and distracted
anyone talking to him. 'They are here
to teach us how to fight,' he replied.
'To fight? Why—' I was incredulous.
'You are very dull.' He was annoyed now.
'And I have better things to do
than answer your questions.'

At that, he grasped a goblet of wine
and walked off to talk to another River God.
I turned to Asteria who looked at me

with an equally bemused expression.
Leto had taken Metis back to their palace
as it was best to keep Metis out of sight.

Asteria's delicate hand was holding
a small chalice of nectar. She sipped it
as we watched the
chaos that was a feast for my family
from a comfortable distance
close to the door. In the centre of the hall,
I could see a throng that included our fathers.
'Is that them?' Asteria gestured.
I followed her gaze to two strangers.

They towered above everyone around them,
dark hair haloed with curls. It was not hard
to tell that they were brothers. One was built
bigger than the other and my guess was this
was Perses, the God of Destruction,
with his huge arms and rippling muscles.
Next to him, the leaner one must be
Pallas, the God of Weaponry.
I started slightly when he looked over,
his amber eyes holding my stare.

I averted my gaze but not before
Asteria noticed what had happened.
'You should speak to him.'
She had a teasing tone. I stared at her.
'And why would I do that?'
'Perhaps because he is making his way over here.'
She chuckled and before I could process
what she had said, she quickly turned
and walked away, just as a deep, rich voice said,

'You must be the Oceanid, Styx.'

Pallas

My sisters often spoke
about Gods and men
in ways of the flesh.

For years, I had ignored
this as unimportant.
But now, I felt strange.

It was like a pull
within me, drawing me
closer toward him.

His dark-bright eyes
never left my face
as he waited for my voice.

I finally found it
and said quietly,
'Yes. I am Styx.'

I searched for more words
but they eluded me
in his presence.

What was wrong with me?
I was usually so
sharp-tongued.

He moved closer.
'You helped Oceanus
build many of his rivers.'

I was surprised by this.
'Did he tell you that?'
Pallas shook his head.

'Your brothers did,
mostly out of resentment.'
I narrowed my eyes slightly.

'I am surprised they told you.'
He shook his head.
'They wouldn't have,

but I was admiring your work
on the great map in
Oceanus's chambers.'

I had to look away at this,
a warmth colouring my face.
When I turned back,

I saw three of my sisters
had appeared at his side.
With their long limbs

and silky dark hair,
they smiled and demurred
to get his attention,

which he readily gave.
They pulled at his hands
leading him away.

I had seen this happen
countless times,
and yet this time,

I felt it like the sting
of fresh salt
on an open wound.

But he turned back
as he was led away,
and offered me a smile.

I did not return it.

'What Did He Say?'

Asteria appeared by my side.
She was still holding her chalice,
but her eyes were brighter
and her mood merrier.

'He asked about the rivers
I helped my father build,'
I said in annoyance.
Asteria fell into step beside me.

'That he takes an interest
in what you do is good,'
she told me quietly.
I stopped walking and turned.

'Why would it matter?'
I asked in annoyance.
'I can see no point
to his interest in me.'

Before Asteria could speak again,
my father's voiced echoed
through the halls.
'Family! Come close!'

The Fateful Decree

Asteria and I walked back
into the great hall as my father's head
swivelled, searching for someone

amongst the throngs of Gods
and nymphs and lesser deities.
When his eyes finally stopped on me,

a strange discomfort gripped my bones.
'Styx,' my father's voice boomed.
'Come forward please, my daughter.'

For a moment, my legs would not move,
until Asteria nudged me forward
and I hesitantly walked toward him.

At his side, Pallas and Perses stood
towering above my parents.
When I reached my father,

he gestured for me to stand
beside him as well. Something
told me I should run.

But I did as I was asked.
'Three nights ago,' Oceanus said,
'I was gifted a prophecy.'

'In it, my oldest daughter Styx
was blessed with four children.'
My heart thudded in my chest

as I stared at my father.
What was he talking about?
The room erupted in whispers.

'All four of these children
will become Gods and be crucial
to the reign of the Titans.'

My mind was reeling.
It felt like the very ichor
inside my body wanted to run.

'According to this prophecy,
she must have a fearless consort,
a God of might unlike any other.

And so, I decree the hand of
my oldest daughter be given to Pallas,
God of Might and Weaponry.'

Applause Broke Out Through the Halls

It was as if the very air inside me
had died and all that was left

was an abyss of confusion.
I stared at my father's face

as he steadfastly looked at the audience.
How could he do this?

How could he expect me to marry
this God I had only just met?

We had not exchanged five sentences.
I looked to Pallas but he was

surrounded by well-wishers.
His brother offered me a kind smile

in his stead. Did Perses already know?
Did no one think to inform *me*?

Was I so very small to my parents
that telling me first didn't matter at *all*?

'No'

The word spilled from my mouth
like the waves of a stormy river.

At first no one looked at me.
So I spoke louder and firmer.

'NO!'
At my near shout, the rejoicing

stopped. My father finally
looked into my blazing eyes.

'I will not be given away
like I am a plaything.'

My words were laced with
the sharp edges of my fury.

'You cannot do this to me.'
My father's eyes turned turbulent

as his gaze upon me became
withering. 'You will do as is asked

of a daughter of the house of Oceanus.'
I glared back at him.

'I am your daughter now, am I?
How convenient for you.

To name me daughter at your pleasure,
but dismiss me when I need you

to be my father.' A gasp rose from
my sisters who stepped back.

My father's mighty dark river,
which ran under the obsidian

below our feet rumbled, a noise
that matched the rage on his face.

'You are unworthy of this honour!'
His voice was so loud now the floor shook.

'But as my eldest child, you will do
as the family needs!'

I opened my mouth to speak again,
to rebuke his words and make him see,

truly see me, for a change.
But a cool hand slipped into mine.

And I knew that it was Asteria
standing at my side.

She met my eyes and I saw
the caution in her own.

Before I spoke again,
she whispered,

'There are many ways to build
a fox. And better ways to fight

oceans than crashing into their waves.'
I squeezed my eyes shut and bit back

the poison-laced words I had
built up inside. Instead, I spoke to Pallas,

who had been standing very still
during my loud and rage-filled outburst.

'May you be a worthier father
than mine has been to his daughter.'

Before anyone could speak
another word, I left the room,

leaving a sea of confused
and angry divinities behind me.

Fury Was Etched in My Bones

Wounded and wilting,
I spent the night in Asteria's room,

her arms holding me tight
as I wept in helpless anger.

I hated my tears, hated that this
was all I had left to show for my rage.

Hated that my father had treated me
like a possession, an object

to be handed over. 'If I was a Goddess,
not a nymph, he would never do this to me.'

My voice was curdled with grief
as I shook in Asteria's arms.

'Goddesses have divine purposes, Styx,
but we too are bound by rules set by Gods.'

My friend was gently running her hands
through my hair, trying so hard to soothe me.

I met her eyes and said softly,
'What are you telling me?'

Asteria shook her head sadly.
'Just that our freedom is an illusion.'

She pressed a gentle kiss to my forehead.
'But what we share, the power we have . . .

that is our own. No one controls that.'
Perhaps I was too unhappy to understand

what she fully meant in that moment.
But instead of responding,

I buried my face in her shoulder
and lost myself in my rage and despair.

Perhaps this was why the dream came to me
that particular night.

Perhaps this was why the prophecy
wormed its way into my mind.

The Dream

I saw myself walking along
my father's dark underground river.
It pulsed and stormed, ink black,
as though threatening me.
But I stood upon its banks
glaring back at it unafraid.

And then, from the abyss,
a large divine face emerged,
the water's violent waves
helping it rise to the surface.
It was the face of a God I did not know.
Bearded, handsome, but with a glint

of cruelty in his eyes. Soon,
the rest of him emerged
until everything around him
was dwarfed. The river,
the riverbanks, myself.
His hand pushed upward

and I realized he was pushing
at the floor of Oceanus's palace.
As his hand pushed, the palace
walls began to fall,
and fall,
and fall . . .

Until finally I awoke,
feeling like his hand
was wrapped around

my own throat. A piercing cry
of fear escaped my lips,
waking Asteria next to me.

'Styx?' Asteria asked with worry.
The look on her face
reflected the fear clawing at my heart.

'Asteria,' I said breathing heavily,
'I did not mean to wake you.'
She shook her head.

'Tell me what you saw.'
Asteria knew the aftermath
of a prophetic dream well enough;

her own came frequently.
'I . . .' I struggled to find words
as she handed me a goblet of nectar.

'My father's palace . . .
Something is . . .
something is coming, Asteria.'

She waited patiently as I gathered
my thoughts. 'It was a God I did not know.
A God emerged and he destroyed—'

The fear closed my throat again.
I took a deep shuddering breath.
'Something is coming for us all.'

Resignation

Asteria's hand clasped mine.
'You are safe here, Styx. And whatever
comes, we can face it together.'

I winced and shut my eyes.
'No. This was . . . this was bigger.
It was something different.'

My hands shook and I looked at them,
Then looked back at Asteria.
'I think . . . I may have to

do as my father has asked.'

Asteria's Home

Unable to face going back to my father's palace immediately or even consider meeting my new consort until I was sure I was ready, I spent my days in Asteria's home with her mother and sister and Metis. Before my eyes, I watched Metis become as tall as the rest of us. Forever fascinated by the world, she would disappear for long walks alone with the fox by her side, bringing home an assortment of strange objects and flowers. It was finally revealed what I had long suspected, that Metis was like Asteria and me; her capacity to create pure white flowers from stones gave this away one morning on the beach. As much as I longed for her to be closest to me, it was Leto she chose to be her confidante, and I often saw them walking across the sands together deep in conversation. Asteria and I visited the forest and gathered herbs and flowers to learn more about them. Why did they die while we lived forever? What were they for? How did they work? I remember those days in Asteria's palace as full of learning and a freedom I never experienced in my own home. If anyone ever asked me, I would never tell them. This was the last time I ever felt truly safe.

A Visit

One night, Asteria, Leto, Metis, and I
returned home long after
Hyperion had set the sun.
Our aunt Nyx now ruled the skies.

We entered the palace
with the cadence of laughter,
our feet stomping together,
flowers braided through our hair.

But as we crossed the main archway,
Coeus was waiting for us.
'I heard you return.' His expression
was unreadable. 'You have guests.'

We looked at one another in surprise,
but I felt a flash of anger in my bones.
My parents must have sent my sisters.
We followed Coeus into his chambers.

There sitting on two gilded chairs
were the two Gods who had
turned my immortal life into a mess.
Perses . . . and Pallas.

It was Perses who cleared his throat.
'Our apologies for the unannounced visit.'
We all stood there waiting for him
to continue.

'But your father
has summoned you
back to the palace for
the joining ceremony.'

I let out a short, incredulous
bark of a laugh. 'I thought
I made my intentions clear.'
Perses's dark eyes, molten gold,

stared at me, then wandered
to look at Asteria by my side.
'Perhaps he thought you would
have changed your mind.'

Asteria took my hand,
and I remembered the dream.
But I did not want to seem like
I was giving in too easily.

'I would like to speak with Pallas.'
At the sound of his name,
Pallas looked me in the eye
waiting for my next words.

I looked at Perses and Coeus.
'I would like to speak to him alone.'
The two Gods hesitated,
but obediently left us.

Leto and Metis
went with them.
Asteria squeezed my hand.
'I am outside the door.'

A Conversation

After everyone else was gone,
I turned to Pallas. I tried to ignore
the way my heart pounded
when his eyes met mine.
The way his dark hair curled
like a halo around
his perfectly chiselled face.

'And do you agree with all of this?'
I asked him quietly.
His handsome face creased
in confusion, then cleared.
He looked down at his hands
(rugged, beautiful hands),
and said gently,

'Styx, I am not good with words.
Hand me adamantine and I will
make you a weapon unlike any other.
But words are not made in a forge
and I do not know what to say.'
He looked into my eyes.
'Our parents have decided.
What else is left?'

I stared at him, disbelieving.
'Is your life forfeit so easily?'
I crossed the room so that
we were closer. 'Look at me!'
I told him, anger and hurt
and fear in my very bones.
'Is this what you want
to be tied to for all eternity?

Do you understand
what it would mean to be wed to me?
Split eyes and coldness,
my sisters say my real mother
is a serpent because I could not have
been born from Tethys's sacred womb!'

He watched me closely.
'Do you see yourself
as such a great burden?'
I opened my mouth with a retort
then bit my tongue to reconsider.
I took the empty seat Perses had left.

'I am under no illusion, Pallas.
My sisters are beautiful.
One of them will suit you better.'
It hurt so deeply to say these words.
But I knew. I knew I was not beautiful.
Not like them. I was a nymph
without beauty, my punishment
for being firstborn.

Pallas shook his head.
'I never saw myself with a consort.
But if I ever had one, I would want
her to be spirited, a companion,
an ally. I want her to challenge me.
Beauty was never my interest.'
I considered his words.

He was so different from the shallow
Gods I had come to know.
Finally, I took a deep breath.
'But what if we cannot learn
to care for each other
as consorts should?
What should we do then?'

Pallas reached out gently
and placed a hand on mine.
'Then we learn how to care
for each other as allies
and friends.' I felt the warmth
of his fingers radiate through
my hand, through my skin.

He spoke to the water
inside my body in a way
I never thought possible.
I looked up into his eyes
and said quietly, 'If I return
with you, it will feel like
my father has won.'

Pallas studied me
with an unreadable expression.
Only those amber eyes
betrayed his own inner turmoil.
'Styx, I will not force you
into being my consort.'

I considered his words.
Then I thought about
the dream I had had
of what was coming
toward us.
What was coming
toward all of the Titans.

I lifted my head high
and took a deep breath.
'I will return with you,
Pallas. And we will learn
to make the best of what
we have been given.'

Asteria

DESTINY AND FALLING STARS

PART IV

Outside the Door

The voices were loud in my mind,
demanding my attention.

O Goddess hear our prayers.
O Goddess please protect us.

The chatter was overwhelming.
When I carried uncertainty,

my Oracles chattered loudly
and I had to close my eyes

to quiet them down.
My head throbbed.

Metis was being impatient.
'What is taking them so long?'

I placed a soothing hand
on her arm. 'Give them time.'

I did not add *especially* Styx.
The three of us knew now

that patience was the only way
to win a place in her heart.

But Metis was easy to anger
and hard to soothe.

She shook my hand off
and said, 'This is not fair.

They should not have come.
Styx did not want to see him.'

Her rage was righteous now,
but I knew Metis well.

I had seen her once destroy
her entire chambers in fury

when my mother had told her
she was to stay in her halls

after she had been caught
trying to listen in to my father

and one of his brother's conversations.
Metis had never liked rules.

Behind me I heard footsteps
and turned to see Perses.

My heart skipped a beat
as his eyes met mine.

His chest was bare and every
sinew and muscle was a work of art.

Suddenly the voices in my head
grew very quiet and I sighed with relief.

'Asteria.' He nodded at me.
'May I have a word?'

Leto and Metis looked at each other
with silent understanding.

'Let us know when they emerge,' Leto said as they left.

Perses

If anyone were to ask me,
I would say it was his hands.
His fingers that were destined
to hold weapons, crush bones,
strong, powerful, but also
somewhere within his veins
there lay a tenderness I could see.

When his molten-gold eyes met mine,
the secrets of a thousand suns
simmered inside them.
He was built to lift mountains,
and each muscle, each plane
of his body told the story of strength.
I cleared my throat – *Be careful, Asteria* –

and asked him with caution,
'How can I help?'

A Proposition

Perses smiled at me and said softly,
'I think we find ourselves in a common
predicament. I have noticed Styx
is close to you. I am close to my brother too.
This decision to wed them
was decided between our fathers,
and my brother is dutiful.
But what I would like . . .'
He lowered his voice as he looked
in the direction of the door.
'I would like to see him content,
instead of simply dutiful.'

I contemplated his words
for some time, then said,
'Styx is my dearest friend,
very much a sister to me.
I too would like to see her content,
instead of forced into an arrangement
not of her choosing.'
He nodded and asked,
'What if we helped them?'
His scent enveloped me,
like the earth after rainfall.

I closed my eyes and composed myself.
'What precisely are you
suggesting we do?'

A mischievous smile
spread across his face.
'Perhaps we find ways
to bring them together.

I believe they have
more in common than
they realize. While they are resigned
to their fate, we can show them
that this fate is not such a terrible thing.
Pallas is partial to fermented
wines, handcrafted objects, and quiet.
What does Styx enjoy?'

I considered this. It was hard
to think with him so close.
'Styx enjoys being away
from Oceanus's palace.
She likes the quiet
and time by the sea,'
I offered in a whisper as
I heard movement behind
the door. 'Ah,' Perses said.
'Perhaps we can arrange
for them to meet on a walk?'

I smiled and nodded
just as the door opened
and Styx and Pallas walked out.

Styx Looked Resigned

I wanted to embrace her,
tell her that fate had a kinder
destiny for her, that Pallas was not
the worst choice of consort.

But I knew this was
about being
bartered by her father
without a second thought.

As soon as she looked up at me,
I took her hands and waited
for her to speak as Pallas
stood with Perses.

Her split eyes were unreadable
as she said, 'I have agreed
to go back to Oceanus's palace.
And to be Pallas's consort.'

I inhaled sharply. Styx had
swallowed her pride to do this.
And I knew how much
that must have cost her.

I turned to Pallas,
his expression betrayed
very little but his eyes
shared his concern.

'Are You Sure, Styx?'

I asked, already in my panicking mind,
trying to think of how to help.

We could run away into the woods
and create our own home.

Stop, Goddess, an Oracle whispered to me.
Remember the prophecy.

To be divine was to heed the Fates.
to be powerless to stop them,

yet still to keep trying.
Styx clutched my hands tight.

'Come with me?' she asked.
'Stay by my side?'

I pulled her into an embrace,
and for once, she did not resist.

'I promise you, I will never leave you,'
I whispered to her fiercely.

'I will be by your side forever.
And you will never have to do this alone.'

The Wedding Feast

What kind of feast honours a love that never was? Oceanus's palace was bursting with dancing deities and divine laughter that filled his grand halls, even his great river sounded more like a babbling brook instead of its monstrous rumbling self. Styx's sisters usually enjoyed a banquet, but that day they were eyeing her with an envy that made them look almost green in the firelight of the stars I had hung across the halls. There was a vibrance in the air that extended everywhere, except toward the two rose-and-violet-covered thrones at the front of the room where Pallas and Styx had taken their honoured seats. Styx looked lovely: I threaded her long green tresses with white flowers we grew ourselves. Her eyes were lined with dark kohl to make them shine bright. Her lips were painted rosy red and her emerald dress was made of the finest silk. Pallas's crimson robes only highlighted his golden skin and sinews. They looked beautiful together. But neither of them was smiling. My heart clenched for them both. There had to be a way to bring them together. I knew Styx would grow to care for kind Pallas with a little help. Next to Pallas, Perses caught my eye. And as my pulse began to race, his handsome face creased to offer me a gentle smile.

A Plan

We met later that night
on the golden sands by the sea.

Perses showed me the dock
where Pallas had his forge.

'If you bring her here tomorrow,'
he said, low-voiced, 'I'll bring

the wine. We will stay and keep
them company awhile,

then slip away.' I recalled
Styx's sorrowful face when

she shut the doors of her chambers,
readying herself for Pallas's visit.

Only a moment later, he had left
her rooms and I understood.

Pallas was not the kind of God
to force himself upon a nymph.

And this, if nothing else,
made me sure of the kind of God

he was, and how, perhaps,
just *perhaps*, he was worthy of Styx.

'Perses?' I asked him as the wind
blew my hair across my face.

He turned to look at me, and as though
on instinct, brushed the strands of hair

away from my cheek.
My breath caught for a moment,

his touch leaving a trail of warmth
on my skin cooled by the wind.

'Apologies,' he said quickly.
'I did not mean to . . . overstep.'

We were quiet, unsure for a moment.
The ghost of his touch lingered on my face

and I tried to focus on our task at hand.
'Do you . . . do you think this may work?'

Perses looked out at the seas,
the waves thrashing against rocks.

'I do not know,' he said finally.
'But we must try. For their happiness.'

The Forge

The next day I asked Styx
to accompany me to Pallas's forge.

'What do we need to go there for?'
she complained as we walked out

of her chambers. 'We have our own
work of making to do.'

I shook my head. 'He is your consort.
Why don't we just see what he makes?

Perhaps he creates things like we do.'
She scoffed at this but kept walking.

The beach was bathed in sunlight,
fresh after a morning storm.

From a distance, I saw Pallas
working with dazzling adamantine.

Next to him, tall and broad-shouldered,
was Perses. He raised his hand in greeting

as we approached.
Pallas glanced up from his work

of beating the adamantine into shape.
Around him iridescent objects

gleamed brightly in the sun.
'What are these?' Styx asked,

but her tone was of curiosity,
not of any kind of malice.

Pallas looked up at her.
'Your father brought me diagrams.

He says they came from prophetic
dreams of the Titans. He calls them

divine weapons.' She reached out
and touched the edge of one,

letting out a harsh hiss when
its sharpness cut through her finger,

golden ichor spilling from it.
Immediately, Pallas was up from his forge

taking her hand in his and examining
the wound. 'It'll heal,' Styx said shortly,

but he was already binding it
with a piece of cloth ripped from his robes.

'It will not heal quickly,' I told her.
'That's what adamantine does.'

Styx looked around at the weapons.
And I saw a shadow pass across her face.

Pallas was still holding her hand.
Her face cleared to something softer and she said,

'Thank you.'
I raised an eyebrow and caught Perses's eye.

He smiled at me and winked.
A warmth came to my cheeks.

Perhaps this was the first of many such
moments between Pallas and Styx.

The Carvings

The next evening,
Perses and I met by the docks.

I had whispered to him yesterday
before leaving that I had a plan.

My heart fluttering,
as I escaped from my father's palace

into Nyx's oncoming darkness.
He was standing watching the sea,

his handsome face looking like
it had been chiselled from

the same ancient stone of the cliffs.
I tried to quell my heartbeat.

'Asteria.' The way he said my name
made it sound like ambrosia itself.

'Perses,' I said softly.
For a second neither of us spoke,

until finally he cleared his throat.
'While seeing you is a gift always,

may I ask what you wanted
to speak about?'

I ignored the way his words
made my spirit rise.

'Your brother enjoys carving, yes?'
At his nod, I carried on.

'Come with me. I will show you
things he can carve and leave for Styx.'

It Began Slowly From There

Styx, whom I had never seen take an interest in anything a male God did, started to visit Pallas at his forge more often. I would watch her stand by him having a brief conversation, before she would return to me and we would walk back to the cave together. Perses and I had arranged the first few times, but after that, she had taken to going alone. Perses, at my instruction, began to ask Pallas to carve things for him – an eel, a fox, a crab. Creatures Styx and I had invented. Then I would leave them at her chamber's window. Inside the cave, I asked Styx to help me make a new kind of precious gem, one of amber, just like Pallas's eyes. Together we magicked it out of pure sea stone. Perses left this for him at his forge, letting him know it was Styx's gift to him. He was delighted with it and placed it within the handle of his newest burnished adamantine sword. And then one day, when Styx, Metis, Leto, and I walked into her room, we found the perfect wooden carving of Styx, sitting on her bed. Pallas had crafted a version of Styx who stood tall, her split eyes burning with passion, each tress of her green hair lovingly carved with tender hands. Her hands held swords instead of sitting in prayer. I watched her face as she turned it over in her hands, her eyes soft and full of admiration. 'Go to him,' I whispered softly. We watched from the balcony of her room as she approached Pallas at the forge he worked at, still holding his carving in her hand. Their eyes met and this time their souls did too, as she pulled him close into a gentle, warm kiss.

A Revelation

Gods believed in prophetic dreams
the way the ocean believed in its waves.
For us, prophecies were a gift and a curse,
the dark knowledge the future was
always advancing upon us.

There was a sort of strangeness
that had descended upon Oceanus's palace.
It appeared that most of the River Gods,
and the Nymphs too, were being visited
by dreams that spoke prophecy.

Each one was the same.
Kronos, the God-King,
standing in front of a door.
When the door opens,
a wailing infant Godling

is handed to him by unseen hands
and he cradles the child. Coos to it.
As the baby wriggles in his arms,
He lifts the struggling infant
to his mouth

. . . *and devours it whole.*

Over and over again,
even the least of the divinities
saw it happen. And then, we heard
it was Kronos's mortals who began to feel
and see these same dreams.

This was deeply unusual.
Kronos's mortals were a docile sort,
and as unhappy as he made the divine,
he liked to keep his mortals happy.
These dreams were a disruption.

Metis one day came to me,
her hands clasped before her,
clever golden eyes worried.
'Asteria,' she whispered softly,
'do you think it is true?

That Kronos is devouring
his children?' I gently held her hand.
'I think it *is* true, beloved.
But you need not worry until
we are told by our parents.'

When the news finally came to us,
that Kronos had devoured
four of his children thus far,
Metis locked herself in her chambers
and wept and wept.

When Leto and I tried to comfort her,
all she sobbed was 'Poor Rhea.'

To Be a Prophet in a Time of Danger

was to sense every movement
within my very bones.

As the voices in my head chattered,
I saw how everyone around me

began to act in stranger ways.
In Oceanus's palace, when I visited,

where carefree laughter once resounded,
voices had become more hushed.

Oceanus himself was scarce in those days.
My father and his other Titan brothers

were frequently in his chambers
and River Gods prevented Styx or me

from entering, so we could not hear
what they were speaking of.

My father would come home
an exhaustion in his eyes,

whilst my mother would fret
after they would speak in secret.

When I thought back to this moment later,
perhaps I should have seen

the darkness that lurked
around the corner.

Perhaps I should have seen
how quickly my world was changing.

How nothing would ever
be the same again.

A Call

With Pallas and Styx now happily united,
my clandestine meetings with Perses
had come to an end, causing a sadness
I could not understand nor speak of.

As Metis and Leto talked to me,
often I did not hear their words,
they would repeat themselves
until finally they gave up.

What was this strange ache
my body was putting me through?
It seemed undivine, unholy.
I could not understand it at all.

Until one twilight, when I was sitting
on the marble steps outside
my father's palace, I looked up
and saw Perses walking toward me.

'Asteria,' he said softly,
'may I please speak with you?'
My heart was suddenly ablaze
with something unnameable.

The sight of him had filled
a thirst deep within my bones.
I stood up from the stairs
and smiled, walking toward him.

'Hyperion has blessed us with beauty.'
He gestured to the rosy and orange sky.
'Shall we walk for a while?'
I nodded, not trusting myself to speak.

We began walking away from my father's
palace. After a few moments of quiet,
Perses spoke softly. 'I have missed you,
Asteria.' I opened my mouth to speak

but he shook his head, his face creased
with what looked like worry and . . . fear?
What could possibly make
the God of Destruction afraid.

'I have not been able to stop thinking
about you in days. When I close my eyes
it is your face I see. When I listen
to others converse, it is your voice I long for.'

He stopped abruptly and turned to look at me.
His golden eyes were gleaming with such
desire, that I felt a flush creep into my face.
'Tell me I am not alone. That you too have

some kind of yearning for me.'
He waited for me to speak.
It was strange how suddenly I found my voice.
That all that unnameable pain of his absence

suddenly had a name. Yearning.
'Perses.' My voice was a whisper.
'Thank you for giving this ache
a name. You are not alone.

The stars I care for will tell you
how well I speak of you at night
when no one else can hear my words.'
For a moment, neither of us spoke.

And then, silently, he stepped closer,
brushing my hair out of my face.
His mouth met mine gently at first
and my hands curled around his neck,

pulling him closer.
Beyond us in Nyx's now darkening sky,
several stars danced, glittering.
A celebration of a love well met.

The Vow

It was my own fault, truly, that I did not
want to keep Perses a secret from my parents.

In fact, I wanted to shout my love for him
from the top of the palace, the cliffs.

But as the eldest daughter,
I knew my first duty lay to my parents.

So I told Perses that I would speak
with my father first and tell him

I had chosen my consort. I went looking
for Coeus in his halls but my mother told me

that he was visiting Oceanus again,
so I ran immediately to his palace gates.

When I arrived at Oceanus's chambers,
I saw my father and the five eldest River Gods

gathered with Oceanus around his great map.
'Father . . .' I said breathlessly, 'I have news.'

I felt the same way I did when I was a child
and I would joyously interrupt my father and uncles.

My father smiled at me widely.
'As do I, daughter.'

I paused, confused. Had Perses
already spoken to him?

Instead, my father gestured to the oldest
of the River Gods, Achelous, a handsome God

who had an ink-dark beard, glittering dark
eyes, and the body of a great bull.

'Achelous has asked for your hand,'
my father told me. 'And I have said yes.'

Anger Coursed Through Me

I had always thought that Oceanus
was callous with his own daughters
but my naivety had led me to believe
he only took them for granted
because there were so many of them.

I never thought my own father would
assume that my eternity was his
to bargain away for favour or family.
But I knew that voicing this now
would lead to nothing good.

Instead of responding, I looked down.
'Forgive me, Father, but I do not feel well.'
I took his stunned silence as an opportunity
to escape this room full of male Gods
and the games they played with our lives.

Quickly, I walked to Styx's chambers.
But upon hearing Pallas's voice inside,
I instead retreated to the seaside,
looking for Perses. Fire made my feet
move faster, the humiliation of being

bartered that way without my permission.
How could he? The shock of it stung
almost as much as the audacity did.
Finally, I saw Perses in the distance
training a spate of young River Gods.

Perses Spied Me and Raised His Hand in Greeting

The sight of him made me feel
like my burden wasn't a burden at all.

I walked over to him, calmer now.
His tall, muscular form moved toward me,

and in a moment, he had swept me up
within his arms, his lips meeting mine.

I let myself melt into his warmth,
savouring him before I tore our world asunder.

When we finally broke apart,
I ran my hand along his jawline,

keeping his gaze. 'I went to speak
with my father. I have news.'

Perses's face creased with trepidation
when he saw from my expression

the anger and sadness I felt within.
'He has already promised my hand

to Oceanus's oldest son.' I felt his jaw
tighten under my caress and his tawny eyes

turned molten hot. 'And how do you feel
about being the consort of Achelous?'

I shook my head. 'I already know
who I want to be with, Perses.

From the moment I saw you,
I understood. I simply did not recognize

what to name that feeling.
I know who I want to spend my eternity with.

I am sure Achelous is a kind God
and will make some Goddess happy.

But that Goddess is not me.'
Perses took my hands in his large ones,

brought them up to his lips tenderly.
'If you are sure. I will go speak

with your father. But only with your
permission.' I nodded slowly, knowing

what would come of this.
It was not my father's temper that concerned me.

Oceanus was the oldest of the Titans.
And he did not like to be crossed.

Especially not by those closest to him.

A Broken Feast

As was customary,
a feast was already being held
in the grand halls.

By the time Perses
finished training
the young River Gods,

it was already in full sway.
Oceanus had not spared
any time preparing

a joining celebration.
Much like Styx,
I found myself

clenched fists at the table
at the front of the hall,
laughing divinities

all around me.
I could not see Styx
anywhere, though.

I had spent my time
getting ready while raging
to Leto and Metis

who now stood
worried by either
side of me.

Oceanus was about to
call the festivities
to a halt to speak

when I saw Perses emerge
from amongst the throng.
His eyes briefly met mine,

a subtle nod of comfort
before he approached
my father and Oceanus.

I stood up from my place
and walked toward them.
'Coeus,' Perses said,

'if I may have a word.'
My father, the God of Intellect,
knew from looking between us

what was about to happen.
The look on his face
alerted Oceanus.

The old God of the sea stood
to his full height
and asked coldly,

'What Is It You Want, Young Perses?'

At the boom of his voice,
a hush fell.

Perses looked unperturbed.
He met my father's and

Oceanus's eyes fearlessly.
'I have come for Asteria's hand.'

My father was about to speak
but Oceanus interrupted.

'You are too late. She is promised
to another. My oldest son.'

Perses looked at me.
'Asteria, is that what you want?'

I hated the way all eyes fell on me.
But I could not let Perses stand alone.

'I wish to be with Perses, Father.'
I addressed him instead of Oceanus.

My father looked deeply uncomfortable,
his eyes moving between Perses and me

and Oceanus. 'Asteria,' he sighed,
'you should have told me before.'

Perses shook his head.
'Please do not blame Asteria.

It is I who took my time asking.'
He turned to Oceanus.

'I mean no disrespect
to your hospitality or home.'

Oceanus was thunderous.
'And yet, disrespect is precisely

what you have brought.
Coeus, tell them your decree.'

But my father merely stood quiet.
He was studying me carefully.

Oceanus spun toward my father.
'Now.' His voice threatened a storm.

'No,' said my father softly.
I stared at him and he gave me

the slightest of smiles.
'My daughter will spend eternity

with a consort of *her* choice, not mine.'
A strange relief filled me at his words.

My faith in him had been restored.
I knew he was not like Oceanus.

Perses bowed his head to my father
and quietly took my hand.

Coeus turned to Oceanus and said,
'I will not force my daughter to spend

her goddesshood with someone
she feels bound to out of duty.'

Oceanus glared. 'My daughters
are dutiful enough to serve my vows.'

My father nodded as I finally saw
Styx and Pallas push their way

to the front of the crowd of deities.
'Perhaps you are satisfied with dutiful

daughters, brother. I would rather have
happy ones.'

A gasp resounded and I realized it was my own.
Oceanus's rheumy eyes were icy

as he said, 'As you value daughters
so much more than vows to brothers,

then take your family and go.
Never shall you enter this palace again.'

My father's face flitted between
anger and heartbreak.

Finally, he spoke. 'As you wish,
brother.' He motioned for Leto,

Metis, my mother, and me to join him.
Perses looked at Oceanus

and I saw the livid fury on the old God's face.
'You may join them, Perses.

Do not show your face here again.'
At these words, I heard a sharp

'Wait.' Pallas stepped out into
the light. 'Perses is my brother.

If he is unwelcome, then so am I.'
Styx moved forward and took Pallas's hand.

'And you, daughter? Will you
display your insolence too?'

Oceanus sounded more bitter than enraged now.
'I am simply doing as you asked, Father,'

Styx said sweetly. 'Standing by my consort.'
I would have laughed at her acerbic wit

if the atmosphere were not so tense.
Oceanus, however, would not let his rage go.

'Go then,' he said, sweeping his arm over us.
'Leave these halls and do not return!'

The assembled Gods made way
as my mother, sisters, and I followed my father out.

Before we left, Coeus turned around
one last time, a look of sadness in his eyes.

'Remember what we know is on the horizon, brother.
If we do not stand together, we will fall forever.'

Coeus, God of Intellect

When we left the palace,
my father turned to Perses and me.
'You have cost me my brother.'
The words were a quiet defeat.
'I hope it is a worthy sacrifice.'

My father's words brought tears
to my eyes. The humiliation
he had faced for our love was huge.
Perses's hand tightened on mine,
giving me strength.

'Asteria's happiness is as paramount
to me as it is to you,'
Perses said quietly. My parents nodded.
'Asteria.' My father addressed me now.
'The home you share with Perses –

make it strong.' He had a faraway look
in his eyes. 'Strengthen its walls.
It must be capable of withstanding
anything.' A chill went through me
as I thought of Styx's prophetic dream.

'We will,' Perses said, unperturbed.
'But first I must take Asteria
to see my parents.'
He looked at Pallas and Styx.
'You should accompany us.'

Crius and Eurybia

Their palace was built upon the clouds.
It was said that Eurybia used the flint
inside her own heart to make its doors,
walls, and windows. That Crius,
God of Constellations, crafted
each statue, each artefact inside
from the burning heart of a dying star.

That their three sons were so powerful
because each of them bore Eurybia's
brute force and Crius's powerful hands,
which he used to wrangle the stars.
When Astraeus, Perses and Pallas's
oldest brother, sent the clouds to carry us,
we felt ourselves lifted and taken

so high into the sky that Styx and I
held on to each other tightly,
sure we would fall into the sea.
But then the clouds parted
and we saw it. A white marble
palace where no palaces should be.
Our consorts took our hands
and helped us down.

We walked together through
the ornate silver gates.
Two figures stood before us.
I tensed and Styx did too,
expecting Eurybia and Crius
to be as cold and dark as their reputations
had depicted them to be.

Instead, two kind old faces
smiled and welcomed us all
with wide open arms.

A Palace in the Clouds

It was only after meeting them
that I realized how strongly Gods relied
on their reputations to be worshipped.

The first question Eurybia asked
Styx and me as Perses and Pallas
spoke to their father was

'My dear ones, I hope my sons
are being kind to you?'
Styx and I looked at each other

and we both smiled at once.
Styx had started smiling so much
more these days and it gladdened

my heart to see. 'Yes. Yes,
they are kind. And good,'
I told her. 'You have raised

them both well.' Eurybia beamed.
'Crius and I are equals. We raised
our sons to see their consorts

the way we see each other.'
Styx answered,
her voice laced with bitterness,

'But I am no equal to Pallas.
I was born a nymph
not a Goddess.'

I glanced at her with sympathy.
Styx would never let this go.
Her ambition was the most

powerful thing about her.
Eurybia shook her head.
'You are a valued member

of this family, Styx.
Pallas would do well to seek your
counsel. I know of the rivers

you helped your father build.'
Styx seemed startled by these
words of praise and my soul

ached for her. She had never
heard such compliments from
elder Gods, from her parents.

Eurybia looked at us both as our consorts returned.
'You will always have a home with us.
Please never feel you are alone.'

It Was Crius, God of Constellations, Who Said the Words

'I hear that you caused quite a stir
in Oceanus's palace with your announcement.'

He was looking at Perses and me.
I felt a flush of embarrassment on my cheeks.

'We did not intend to do so,' Perses said.
'But we are now banished forever.'

Crius, to my surprise, only laughed.
'Oceanus has a propensity for theatrics.'

Styx spoke now, her eyes narrowing.
'He was justified in seeing the breaking

of a pact of marriage to one of his own sons,
my brother who is a River God, as an insult,

but he was not justified in his actions.'
Surprisingly, Styx was still defending her father,

but her loyalty toward me held true too.
In my hurry to be with Perses, I had not

considered how deeply this would affect her.
How it would fray her already difficult

relationship with her father.
I reached out and took her hand gently.

'Thank you for leaving with us,'
I said to her sincerely.

Crius Cleared His Throat

'There may be more to Oceanus's decree,'
he murmured, stroking his long beard.
'There have been dangerous whispers
in the winds. Something is coming.'

Pallas and Perses stared at Crius.
'What do you mean?'
Pallas asked him cautiously.
'What whispers do you speak of?'

Crius looked hesitant. He exchanged
a look of trepidation with Eurybia.
'Have the prophetic dreams not visited
any of you?' The look on Styx's and my faces

told him that we had all been having
strange dreams too. Crius lowered
his voice and moved forward.
'Kronos has always been haunted

by the words of Ouranos, who said
that his reign would be cut short
by one of his own children.
Back then, we had all believed

that this was said by the old God
in spite for Kronos turning on him,
taking the sickle to him
and reducing him to half the God

he once was.' Crius's face creased
with worry that made him look
ancient. 'We had thought
that upon wedding Rhea, upon

actually holding his firstborn,
he would change. None of us thought
that he would—' He paused, unable
to speak the truth about his brother.

He leaned back and drank long
from his goblet. 'I fear . . .'
he said quietly, 'that a madness
like this one cannot be cured or forgiven.'

A Promise

We all rested uneasily once Hyperion
had set the sun and Nyx was out
painting the sky black again.

When Perses finally slept, I crept out
of the chambers we shared
and knocked softly

on Styx and Pallas's door.
To my relief,
it was Styx who opened it.

'We must talk,' I told her urgently.
She nodded and left the room.
We headed to the balcony

that overlooked a silver moon
nurtured by my mother, the clouds
reflecting its glow against a midnight sky.

'Styx,' I asked her, 'do you know
what fear feels like?' Styx stared at me.
'We are immortal. What do we have to fear?'

I took a deep breath. 'Do you remember
when we first met in the cave,
and I got trapped underwater?'

Styx nodded, our first meeting
was seared into both our minds.
'I pictured an eternity,'

I began softly. 'I pictured an eternity
trapped there, in the water,
with no one to free me or speak to.

I imagined never tasting nectar again,
never knowing love, or seeing the sunlight,
imprisoned forever underwater.

We may be immortal, Styx,
but there are still ways to hurt us. What is
immortality if we have to spend it alone?'

'Asteria, I had known loneliness
a long, long time before I met you.
I know its pain well.'

She reached out and took my hand.
'As long as we are together,
nothing will ever happen to you.'

I squeezed her hand for comfort,
then asked her,
'Can we make a promise?'

Styx nodded.
'No matter what happens
between us, we will look after

the children we will have one day,' I said.
Styx's eyes filled with tears.
'Asteria . . . I would never let harm

come to your child.'
She put her arms around me,
a rare thing for her to do. 'I promise.'

For the first time in a long time,
I let my body loosen. Letting go of all
the fears I had been carrying for so long.

And the voices in my head
became a soft hum
instead of a cry in the dark.

The Message

Styx and I spent the night talking
about how our lives had changed.
We tried not to speak of the unknowns
that were facing us both,

instead considered only the possibilities
now that we were consorts of two brothers.
'We can make our own family,'
Styx told me. 'And it will be kind.'

I agreed. 'Our children will be good
to one another and not hurt one another.
We will not play the strange games
that other Gods play.'

Perhaps it was naivety. We were
young, determined our friendship
would form the basis of our families.

Perhaps it was hope. That we
could build a more beautiful thing
than what we had been given.
But the next day,

when we all met together in the halls
where their parents had laid
a morning feast, I saw him.
One of my father's messengers.

There was a grave look on Eurybia's face.
She turned to me and said,
'Your father has asked for you
to return at once.'

I frowned. What could possibly
have happened in the short time
I had been away?
And then, Crius said words

that chilled me to my very bones.
'You sister Metis has disappeared.'

Styx

OF SISTERS AND SEARCHES

PART V

Dread

For years, I had feared this.
Since Metis was an infant,
I had feared that one day
she would disappear,

just as quickly as she appeared.
I cannot explain why this thought
had rooted within me for so long.
Perhaps it was because we held

the secret of her birth away from her.
Perhaps it was because
we had never stopped lying to her
about whose sister she really was.

A ghost of a prophecy had wrapped itself
around my mind:
One day she will learn the truth.
And then she will leave us all.

I looked at Crius's face blankly,
then turned to Asteria's worried one.
'We have to go find her.
We have to go *now*.'

Questions

Pallas and Perses knew better
than to argue with Asteria or me
when we decided on something together.

They knew our bond to each other
meant more to us than any other.
Immediately, they summoned

Astraeus's clouds, and together,
we left to return to the palace of Coeus.
My heart pounded as I considered

all the places my sister could go.
I came up empty. Metis was secretive
and only close to Leto.

'Perhaps,' Asteria said reading my mind,
'Leto has the answers we are looking for.'
A surge of bitter envy ran through my veins.

Metis had always been closest to Leto
in a way that made me ache.
And perhaps Asteria was right.

Leto might have some of the answers
that we so desperately needed.
But if this was true then why had her sister

allowed Metis to leave at all?
I knew there was much more to this.
A child who grows up as a secret

eventually chooses the only way possible
for her. She becomes secretive herself.
Or she disappears.

An Aftermath

Nyx had already wrapped the sky in her cloak
by the time we returned to Asteria's parents' palace.

The silence in those halls as we walked them
was as haunting as a siren's song.

Every step we took echoed
as though a thousand voices sang.

Pallas held my hand and I realized
I was trembling.

Was this fear? Was this anger?
When we reached the doors of Coeus's chambers,

we heard the voices of Coeus and Leto within.
Quickly pushing the doors open,

we went into the unknown.

Leto's Despair

Perhaps I would have been more enraged
at her had she not immediately rushed to us,
weeping. She fell into Asteria's arms apologizing.

'I should have been watching her! After what she
learned about Rhea and Kronos, she was never
the same.' Leto mourned, holding Asteria tight.

'Leto,' Coeus said quietly,
'give them time to ask their questions first.'
As ever, Asteria's father was omniscient.

'How could this have happened?' I demanded,
Pallas's hand tightened around mine.
'How could she just disappear like this?'

The room felt so still after I said these words.
As though no one wanted to admit the truth
until I had said out loud. Metis was *gone*.

Leto wept harder into Asteria's shoulder.
'I am sorry, Styx, I wish I—'
'I have no time for your wishes,' I snapped.

'We need to know where she's gone.'
Coeus turned to me now, a frown
on his face. 'It was not Leto's fault.'

'Whose was it then?' I turned to him.
A chill fell between us.
'It was mine.'

What Metis Heard

My mind whirled with a thousand questions.
What did he mean it was his fault?
I glared at him, my voice a hiss. 'Explain.'

He sighed, then walked to the window where Phoebe,
his wife, was in the skies holding the moon,
its light shining onto the sea and onto these onyx floors.

'My banishment from Oceanus's palace
had laid claim to much of my mind.
I was not thinking clearly who heard me.

Metis was in the hallway, about to enter
my chambers, when she heard me say
the words, that I had protected *him*

by taking her in. I did not know she
had heard me until she entered and asked,
"Am I not yours, Father?"'

My heart stopped and I felt as though
every drop of ichor was drained from my body.
The terrible secret we had kept from her was out.

Metis knew.

How to Find a Lost Goddess

First, you must know why a Goddess becomes lost. A secret is kept from her. A story of her origin hidden in the dark. A tale that should be beautiful is buried, out of sight, hidden inside a dark cave. There are many ways to lose a Goddess. Many ways to lose a sister, a daughter, a friend. You must admit that you have created her despair. You must know the path that this will lead her to take is one that is far away from you. To find her, you must make amends. To find her, you must admit that you are to blame. That a nymph who becomes a Goddess has a different path in an immortal life. That a daughter kept secret will eventually learn her truth. To find her, learn the map of the seas, the stars, and the soil. Goddesses know well how to disappear when they do not wish to be found. This is what women and Goddesses share in common. Women get lost all the time. Did no one ever tell you this tale? Who else do you think is singing to you in the dark?

Lessons in Cartography

It was Perses who spoke in the end.
Perses who saw what we needed was hope.
He took Asteria's and Leto's hands
and made a promise to them both.

'We will find her. We will bring her home.'
Pallas held me while I wept.
Did Metis blame me too?
Did she know I knew the secret

and kept it from her too?
She was the only Oceanid sister
I had ever loved and I had never told her
for I thought it would keep her safe.

Now she was gone, and all I wanted
was to let her know this was all for her.
That keeping her a secret protected her.
Pallas spoke quietly. 'We need a map.'

Coeus turned to him. 'A map of where?'
Pallas smiled. 'Everywhere.'
Coeus folded his hands,
and from between his fingers appeared light.

He drew in the air, the beam gleaming
in the darkness of the chambers,
and he showed us his map of the seas,
the stars, and the soil.

They Kept It in Memory

The others were Gods
and Goddesses and
they had the ability to burn
this light and air map
into their memory.

But because I was a nymph,
my heart moved to smaller things.
I told Asteria, 'Before we leave to look
for Metis, we must take care
of all that we have loved and made.'

Asteria understood quickly.
We turned to our consorts.
'Give us till the morning.
We have some tasks we must do,'
I told Pallas and Perses.

They looked as though they had
a thousand questions. They looked
as though they wanted answers.
But perhaps the determination on our faces
told them that we would never say.

We would always choose each other first.
And so, hand in hand, Asteria and I
left the palace of Coeus
to finish tending to everything
we had made, our secret gifts.

The Beginning and the End

It was the cave that we visited first.
Our sanctuary where everything had begun.

The place where my eels swam.
Where Asteria's glowworms shone.

Where I had made crabs and we
had made starfish together. Everything breathed

here inside the dark and luminous light.
Tenderly, I raised my eels in small

saltwater circles in my hands and took them to
the wide waters of the sea to set them free.

Asteria gently filled her hands with
the glowworms that shone, and said a prayer

allowing them to breathe easy in the wide seas.
There was ritual here. In releasing all we loved

into the oceans: the starfish, the eels,
the crabs, and the glowworms. We knew

before we had finished, this was the end
of everything we had known as

our favourite hiding place and sanctuary.
Everything we had known of our girlhood.

The Starfox

She was Asteria's, made from fire and the burning heart of a star. She was built from chaos and the sky and all things living and dead. She was fire, but she was also the love and the secret of creation we shared with each other. Asteria wanted so much to bring her with us. A glowing starfox moving across the skies, showing us the way. But I asked her, how would we explain her to Pallas and Perses? What answer would we have to give them of her origin? And Asteria was broken-hearted, but she understood. It was time for the starfox to have a new home, for others to look after her instead of us. So, to my youngest Oceanid sisters, who were still kind, whose competitive attributes had not overshadowed their soft nature, we gave the starfox as a gift. I knew one thing about Oceanids: we cared for all things living, nurtured them well. My littlest sister had turned her wide, luminous brown eyes to me and asked, *But what about her mate? Does she not need a friend?* Asteria, whose heart was already in pieces, immediately went into the deep woods and returned a while later with a bright rose-and-azure-coloured starfox. As we watched the two foxes play with each other, bright amber-and-rose embers sparking from their tails, we had held hands and tried to remember that here, in every ending, there was a soft, small beginning. For everyone who cared to see it, it would serve them well. Asteria and I made a promise to each other then. We would not practise magic in front of our consorts. No one must know of this secret power we held. This was for us, and only ourselves.

Dawn

When rosy-fingered Eos
rose across the horizon
and soft gilded light fell
across the oceans and all
the secrets they held within,

Asteria and I returned to the palace
to find Leto, Pallas, and Perses
waiting for us upon the stairs.
Asteria's parents were nowhere to be seen.
Leto told us, 'They do not want us to go.'

I hissed at these words,
'It is not their choice to make.
We will go where we please.'
Pallas gently took my hand.

'I promise we will find her,'
he told me, his amber eyes
like molten-hot liquid,
filled with the promise
of hope and love.

I smiled tiredly at him
and turned to Perses.
'How will we travel?'
Perses looked over the horizon.
'Our brother Astraeus's children,

the Anemoi.'

The North Wind, Boreas

We had no ship to aid us,
no waters we could tread,
but we had four winds to carry us.
The first of which appeared
not long after Perses spoke.

Unlike his uncles,
Boreas was thin and icy,
his long beard, blue
like his lands in the north.
He arrived in a chill before us.

A ship made of clouds brought him.
'Perses. Pallas.' He spoke briskly,
like the ice cold that made him.
He bowed politely to us.
'Aunts, as requested, I bring some news
of your missing sister.'

I was deeply impatient
and said shortly,
'Enough ceremony, speak quickly.'
He raised his eyebrow at Pallas,
but Pallas simply took my hand,

caressing it gently to show support.
'There has been word of your sister
visiting Tartarus. She was looking
for answers within the Underworld,
asking questions built in riddles.

Only the great Tartarus knows
where she went after this.'

I gasped. *Oh Metis, what are you doing?*
But to him I simply said,
'Can you take us there?'

He nodded thoughtfully.
'I can take you to the entrance
of Tartarus. The rest you must
do alone.' I thanked him curtly,
and he gestured to his ship.

'Come then,' he said softly,
'let me take you to the mouth
of the Underworld.'
There we would meet
Tartarus, both place and God.

Asteria's Intuition

Boreas's vessel was made of ice and snow,
and even though we were immortal,
our bodies designed for eternal life,
we were creatures used to the hot sand
of my father's shores,

where Hyperion's sun was plentiful.
This vessel was shaped like what
Kronos's mortals called boats,
but it was large enough to carry
a hundred immortals.

While Leto, Pallas, and Perses conferred
with Boreas, Asteria came to me,
wrapping a warm sheepskin
around my bare shoulders.
'Thank you,' I told her in relief.

As we passed through the clouds,
looking over the seas, Asteria
asked me softly, 'Why did you
not tell me, Styx?' I stared at her,
unable to fathom her words.

She looked down at my stomach
and my eyes narrowed in understanding.
'How did you know?' I demanded.
I had been so careful even Pallas
had not noticed the slight swell

of my belly. Asteria took my hand.
'I am the Goddess of Oracles, Styx.
And I know you better than anyone.'

I sighed and held her hand tight.
'Then you must promise not to tell him.'

I looked over to Pallas, his forge-worn hands
animated as he spoke to his nephew.
'He worries. He would not let me
come on this journey if he knew.'
Asteria raised an eyebrow. 'Pallas?'

Her eyes danced with amusement.
'As if any God or immortal could ever
stop you from doing something you want.'
I smiled wryly at her words as she added,
'You do not even allow your father that.'

We both laughed at this, the sound
tinged with a certain sadness now.
We had both been banished for this.
For our insolence of valuing our freedoms
and each other over commands.

I looked to Asteria, my gaze soft.
'Do not tell him. I will. I need time.'
She smiled at me and tilted her head.
'But you must tell him soon,'
she said, looking at my belly.

Before I could respond, Boreas spoke.

'We Have Arrived'

It was as though we were slowly
falling out of the sky toward the ground.
Asteria and I both swayed, holding

each other's hands tighter than ever.
The cold body of the vessel began to dissolve,
and I could see mist rising around me.

By the time our feet touched the hot earth,
the entire vessel had disintegrated into mist.
As it cleared, a large cavern glowed before us,

a hundred rivers of magma flowing inside.
I could see why it was called the mouth
of Tartarus. The entire cavern looked

like it was a molten hot maw
of a monster made of rivers of fire.
Asteria gripped my hand hard.

'For Metis,' she whispered,
as Leto, Perses, and Pallas joined us.
Boreas looked upon us as though afraid,

then disappeared up into the clouds.

Tartarus

There were only two realms
to the Underworld.

Where the mortals went,
and where the immortals went.

But where the immortals went
was not just a place, but also a God.

What else could keep the divine
clenched between its teeth?

A cage would never hold us,
we would find a way out of it.

But Tartarus, the son of Chaos,
brother of Gaia, Eros, Erebus, and Nyx,

was both the cage and the weapon,
like a terrible womb filled with

a thousand immortal lives,
a burning inferno that captured forever.

We walked into the mouth of the cave
and within moments, we heard a roar.

'Children of Titans.
You are not welcome here.'

Tartarus Rose from the Rivers of Fire

His body was carved from dark volcanic rock,
ashes made up his face, glowing, molten magma
formed his limbs, his torso, his eyes.
It was as though the very earth came together
to create him, this fearsome beast of a God.

He was ancient, more ancient than time itself,
and his massive body spoke of things
we would never understand as newer Gods.
For a second, no one spoke. Then Perses
stepped forward and said quietly,

'Uncle, we have need of your aid.'
At his heart, Perses was a strategist.
As God of Destruction, he was fearless.
The rest of us glanced at one another,
and it was I who spoke up next.

'The other child of Titans who visited you.
The one with yellow eyes like mine.
Where did she go?' I eyed the behemoth
we called an uncle. For some time
he did not say a word. Then,

'I will answer your question
if you answer mine.' I took a deep breath,
but it was Asteria who spoke next.
'We will do our best, uncle.'
And we all waited for what he said.

'How Many Years Does a God Live?'

What a strange question.
It felt like it had an obvious answer.
The ancient being before us
was watching us intently, magma-filled eyes
gazing on us all at once.

Perses tried his answer first.
'An eternity,' he said quietly.
The great God shook his head.
'An uncountable number of years?'
Leto suggested hesitantly.

He shook his head again.
Pallas spoke after that.
'As many as Chaos allows.'
Tartarus gave a rumbling
chuckle but shook his head.

Asteria spoke now, softly.
'As many as the stars.'
He smiled this time, but shook
his head again.
'You have one more chance.'

He turned to look at me.
'It is yours, little one.'
I took a deep breath and spoke quietly,
my heart thudding in my chest.
'As many as he or she is remembered.'

Tartarus Laughed

and nodded happily.
He turned to the others.
'We are a hubristic race.
We believe ourselves immortal,
but we rely on being evoked.

Only a nymph amongst Gods
can answer this question honestly.'
He looked to me,
now filled with gentleness.
'What is it you want, little one?'

I swallowed hard.
'Metis, the other Titan Goddess
who visited you. Where did she go?'
Tartarus narrowed his eyes slightly,
as though digging through memory.

'She was looking for a lava stone.
She too answered a riddle for it.
Then asked me where the garden
of the golden apples lay.'
I frowned at his words.

The garden of the golden apples?
It was Pallas who took my arm then.
'He is speaking of the king of orchards, Atlas.'
I looked at the great being and whispered,
'Thank you.'

The West Wind, Zephyrus

Leto and Asteria hugged me close
as we left our strange uncle and the Underworld.
My face was hot from recognition.
The first time an ancient God had seen my mind.

Pallas took my hand as we walked
down to the edge of the volcano of Tartarus.
He smiled at me and whispered,
'You were always the cleverest of us.'

I felt a smile tug at my lips.
His pride in me was unwavering,
and his belief in me was so powerful.
He lifted my hand and kissed it.

When we reached the edge of the shore,
the sea lapping at our feet,
Perses raised his hands to his mouth and
a strange siren-like call escaped his lips.

It raised a cry from the birds above.
And soon, a soft breeze surrounded us and
a young, bright-eyed God was before us.
He was little more than a youth

with curly hair that fell into his eyes.
'Hello, uncles and aunts,'
he said with a merry smile.
'Where shall we go?'

'We Must Go to See the King of the Orchard'

Perses told his jovial nephew.
I was already feeling tired just looking
at the youth. He seemed like someone
Asteria and Leto might find more palatable.

Zephyrus had a wide smile for us all
as he sang, 'A journey through
the clouds for one and all it is.'
And a cloud appeared under our feet.

Unlike Boreas's sturdy cold vessel,
this was a haphazard but warm cloud
that lifted us from the shore and above
until we were travelling through the air.

The infant within my belly
also disliked this means of travel,
and in a few moments, I had to sit.
The cloud held me like a cushion.

Asteria sat next to me
as Pallas looked upon me curiously.
'Is all well?' she asked me quietly.
I nodded to her as I heard Zephyrus

say to his uncles, 'This is the best
way to travel, is it not? Sailing
through the air on a cloud?'
I vehemently and thoroughly disagreed.

A Dark Question

As we rose through the air,
closer and closer to darkness,
Asteria whispered to me,
'Why did she want it?'

The strange feeling in my womb
kept me deeply preoccupied
and it took me some time before
I could answer her.

'What do you speak of?'
We watched as the stars cleared
as we travelled along the top
of the sky.

'The lava stone,' Asteria said. 'Why did
Metis go all the way to Tartarus for it?'
It was a question that had
also crossed my mind.

A dark thought ran through my head
but I shook it clear. 'I do not know.'
My words were slow in formation.
I did not add the rest aloud:

And I am not sure I want to find out.

The Orchard

At the top of the sky, beyond the clouds, just before the azure meets the midnight of Chaos, there lies an orchard. This is not an orchard like the ones mortals know. The trees are not quite trees, and the fruit is not quite fruit. Instead, it is an orchard where the trees are stardust and the fruit is the stars that we have come to know so well. It is said that the father of these stars, the maker, is the great gardener of the light. He sits in the middle of this strange orchard, his large loving hands gently picking up star after star to examine it, halfway between the heavens and Chaos, in this liminal nowhere place where he plants stardust tree after stardust tree. This orchard is one of many, but it is his favourite, because it is the first. His name is Atlas. Father of constellations and stars, the great gardener of the universe.

As We Got Closer, Atlas Turned to Look at Us

'Young Zephyrus,' Atlas, the giant
in the middle of this strange
orchard of light and darkness, acknowledged.
Zephyrus bowed ridiculously low
and said, 'I bring you visitors, uncle.'

Zephyrus's cloud dissipated
as we landed on the azure top
of the skies. We stood there,
unable to understand how
we could stand in such a place.

'It's the stars.' Atlas read our minds.
His voice was a gentle rumble.
Kind-eyed with silver curls,
Atlas was known for his placid ways.
To nurture stars awake,

one must know how to sing
lullabies, and lullabies are not loud.
They are a soft hum in the dark.
A hum that Atlas sang to us.
'The stars' energy built this orchard.

That's why Gods can stand here.
If every star left this place,
we would fall into the oceans below.'
Asteria stepped forward,
her eyes shining bright.

Asteria was the Goddess
of Falling Stars. Atlas made them.
'I have always wanted to meet you,'
she told him with awe. Atlas extended
a large hand and gently placed it

on Asteria's shoulder.
'You have been kind to my stars, niece,'
he said tenderly. 'They told me
you have guided their siblings
to their endings well.'

Asteria's eyes shone and I could not
help but smile too. To be told
you did your loving work well
was a gift not many younger Gods
received from older deities.

She took a moment to compose
herself and asked softly,
'Uncle, did our sister Metis
come here to you?'

Atlas moved his hand to his chin
as though in deep thought.
'She did. She was looking for
the seed of a stardust tree.'

I stared at him.
Why would she need this?
It dawned on me in that moment.
Metis was collecting ingredients.
Asteria and I stared at each other.
Wordlessly, language became realization.

Metis was making a spell.

I Had Always Known She Was Different

Treated as an unholy secret
when she was born,
turned into a Goddess
by virtue of a strange fate,
I had always known

that Metis was destined
for other things. Like me,
she was born with ambition.
Like me, she was strange-faced,
But with white hair and yellow eyes.

All those years spent with Asteria and me,
as we worked and made strange things,
eels and starfoxes, crabs and starfish,
turning flowers into pastes
and learning a nameless art,

we always thought Metis and Leto
were simply sitting there observing.
Glad to be with us while we made
a strange alchemy happen.
Leto *was* observing.

But Metis?
Metis was *learning*.
She was my sister
in countless ways.
How did I not see *this*?

'Why Must You Find Her?'

The question broke Asteria and me
out of our reverie of realizations.

It was Leto who answered.
Sweet Leto who was so patient

with all of us, but most of all
with Metis who was her dearest friend.

'We are her sisters and we want to know
why she disappeared without telling us.'

Atlas looked far away into Chaos's darkness.
'Your sister has her own path.

Just like my brothers have their own path.'
Leto shook her head and said,

'She would never leave without telling me.
She has to have had a good reason.'

Atlas's silver brow furrowed
then cleared as he said,

'I will help you, on a condition.
That if you find her, you do not

destroy what she is building.'

Conditions

I was a nymph. My whole existence
was conditional to the whims
of the Gods, as I had learned.

But for the others,
conditions were a peculiarity.
Pallas and Perses both startled at this.

'But what if she is doing something
that threatens the order of things?'
asked Perses, his deep voice rumbling.

Asteria stared at him as though
seeing him in a different light
for the very first time.

Atlas gave him an unexpected smile.
'If she is disturbing the order
of things, then perhaps the order

is meant to be disturbed.'
At this, all three male divinities
looked perplexed.

But Leto, Asteria, and I understood
precisely what Atlas was suggesting.
Our fates were already written.

Metis could only do
what her destiny demanded.
Fate was inescapable, even for Goddesses.

I raised my head to look at Atlas.
'If it is meant to be,' I said quietly,
'we will not stop her.

Please tell us where she is.'
Atlas thoughtfully picked
a star from a nearby tree.

'You must travel
to the place where the light
and the darkness meet.'

Another riddle. I sighed.
Was this entire journey
simply full of riddles?

Even the child in my belly
did not appreciate this.
I turned to look at the others.

But it was Zephyrus
who spoke up.
'You must call for Notus.

He is the only one who knows
the precise point
of the nocturnal and diurnal feast.'

And with this, he disappeared.

The South Wind, Notus

Pallas called for him
with a horn made from adamantine.
He raised it to his lips and a haunting
song escaped its hollow insides.

The sound that returned was a storm's call,
the rush of wind between clouds,
and then, the grey swirls of a hurricane
made its way toward us.

For a moment, every tree in the orchard
shook and even Atlas's calm demeanour
seemed a little perturbed.
The hurricane stopped at our feet,

disappearing to reveal
a boy scarcely more than a child.
He had grey hair like his hurricane
and the ashen eyes of a storm's heart.

He stared up at his uncles
and then scowled. 'What is it?'
Pallas gave him an indulgent smile.
'You are needed.'

'Oh,' the boy said sulkily,
'I did not expect you to call upon me
at this time. I was raining down on a
village with a perfect thunderstorm.'

Now this irritable nephew of Pallas and Perses
was a child after my own heart.
'Notus,' Perses said to him, more impatient
than Pallas, 'we need you to take us

to where the bright-dark feast is held.'
The boy grumbled but raised his hand,
and a small hurricane expanded into
one so large it looked terrifying.

Perhaps I was mistaken about this boy.
The idea of travelling by hurricane
did not seem all that appealing.
But as the others stepped inside,

Pallas held out his hand to me,
the last of us outside the stormy winds.
I turned to look at Atlas, who smiled at me.
'Thank you, great one,' I said.

And with that, I walked into
the hurricane's swirls,
hoping that this would be
the only time I travelled this way.

A Revelation

Of the three ways we had travelled
by the winds of the Anemoi,
without a doubt, the hurricane
was the most unfriendly of all.

Notus was the youngest of them,
so it stood to reason why his means
of transport was as young and impetuous
as he was. But for me and the child

I carried, the eye of the hurricane
did not spell calm as the grey and white
whipped around us so quickly it made
my head spin. Notus pointedly ignored

all of us as he worked, so Pallas
came to sit by me. 'Styx.'
I kept my eyes closed to abate
the strange feeling within my womb.

'You do not seem yourself.'
His words were like iridescent pearls
coated in worry and care.
I took a deep breath and said,

'I am weary, that is all.'
But when he did not answer,
I turned to look at him.
'Styx,' he said more urgently,

his eyes travelling down
till they landed on my swelling womb.
I shifted so the drape of my clothes
hid my secret a bit better.

But it was too late. His eyes
widened as he looked at me.
'You did not tell me.
Why did you not tell me?'

It was the pain in his tawny eyes
that made me realize perhaps
I had been wrong to keep this
secret from him.

Pallas had been nothing
but kind to me. He was nothing
like my father or brothers.
But my fear of being controlled,

of being told what to do,
had spoken louder than our love.
'Pallas . . .' I started to say,
but Notus interrupted before

I could explain . . .

'We Have Arrived'

The boy-God's hurricane
crackled with unspilled rain
as he brought it to a standstill.

He was the first to step out
of the grey-and-white swirl.
Perses and Asteria followed.

I could not turn to face Pallas,
but I knew him well enough
to expect that disapproval would be

etched into the lines of his kind face.
I felt him shift beside me.
Felt him stand up and then,

despite everything that had
just transpired between us,
he helped me to my feet.

Leto looked to us
and I smiled reassuringly at her.
I knew my relationship with Leto

had been one of tolerance.
But here on this journey
she had proven herself to be

an ally in so many ways.
She smiled back at me gently.
Then Leto, Pallas, and I

walked out into the unknown.

Where Night Meets Day

Halfway between the world, in the middle of the sky, hidden from the eyes of mortals and immortals alike, is an impossible hall. Its arches and pillars are made from storm clouds and hurricanes. Its floor is the midnight blue of the night and the dome is made of the sun's rays, bathing it in a golden hue. At the centre of this hall is a long trapeza laden with chalices of nectar, full plates of ambrosia, the finest of golden apples and crimson pomegranates, honeycomb and cheese, meat marinated in the most delicious of spices and cooked well. Every morning, this was where it was decided that day would follow night. Every evening, they would conclude the opposite. But the two Gods who sat on either end of the trapeza met here always to continue this row. On one side sat burly, yellow-bearded Hyperion, his eyes bright like the sun he was known for, a constant smile on his face. On the other sat the most terrifying and mysterious of all the Primordial Gods, Nyx – her dark hair loose and filled with glowing stars, her onyx skin glowing dangerously in the subtle light of the hall as her black eyes glittered with story and spite.

Nyx, Goddess of the Night

There was a reason why Asteria and I
spoke of her in reverent voices.

Amongst all the Goddesses,
Nyx stood alone in the fear

she inspired amongst the Gods.
Even my father, eldest of the Titans,

was so terrified of her, he winced
whenever her name was brought up.

Oh, to be able to strike fear like that
just by the sound of your name.

It was a thing I could only dream of.
I, relegated to nymph, when I could be so much more.

When we entered, Nyx turned and boomed,
'CHILDREN OF TITANS. WHAT BRINGS YOU

TO THE SACRED HALLS OF NIGHT AND DAY?'
And even Perses, with all his valour,

suddenly looked lost for words
in front of the great, ancient Night.

A Nymph Amongst Gods

Frozen, none of us spoke.
Hyperion, our jovial uncle,
finally cleared his throat.

'Well?' he asked, looking at Notus,
who just shrugged impudently,
then disappeared into a storm cloud.

Wise child, I thought wryly.
Why bother to stay in such
precarious situations if you could escape?

I looked to Hyperion, not daring
to gaze upon Nyx. 'We are looking
for a Titan, one like us.

Atlas told us she came to see you.'
Nyx's booming voice resounded.
'YOU ARE SEARCHING FOR YOUR SISTER.'

I turned slowly to face her.
Of course she would know.
She was the first of Chaos's children,

the oldest of all. She knew
that Metis was Oceanus's daughter.
Her eyes glittered as she looked at me.

'SHE WAS HERE.'
From the corner of my eye,
I saw Hyperion shift uncomfortably.

Then he said to Nyx quietly,
'I told you that no good would come
of giving that child the apple.'

Hyperion was the only God capable
of looking Nyx in the eye.
Not because he was as powerful as her,

but because they had to work together.
For this, he needed a daily courage.
Nyx's eyes narrowed slightly at him.

'I DO NOT RECALL ASKING
YOUR PERMISSION TO GIVE
HER ANYTHING.' He grew quiet.

I spoke up quickly, before I lost
my own courage to speak.
'Please tell us where she went.'

Nyx looked at me,
then at Asteria. 'COME FORWARD.'
All five of us moved to approach her,

but she shook her head and pointed
at me and Asteria.
'JUST YOU TWO.' The others stepped back.

For what felt like a long time,
she simply gazed at Asteria and me,
as we stood in awe before her.

Then she said thoughtfully,
'IN EVERY GENERATION
THERE ARE SOME LIKE US.'

Asteria and I exchanged a quick glance.
We knew she meant our strange powers.
Our consorts, however, did not.

Finally, as though her appraisal
of us had borne some truth to her,
she said, 'YOUR SISTER . . .'

she paused, her eyes contemplating.
'YOUR SISTER ASKED FOR
A GOLDEN APPLE. SHE NEEDED

ITS SEEDS. METIS TOLD ME
SHE WAS GOING TO AIGAION.'
I was startled by this. No God lived there.

'To Aigaion? Why would she go—'
Nyx raised her hand. 'YOU HAVE
YOUR ANSWER. IT IS TIME TO LEAVE.'

Even I, with all my impatience and ire,
did not have it in me to question
the Goddess of the Night.

The East Wind, Eurus

At the edge of the hall
of the nocturnal and diurnal feast,
my body ached with fatigue
and I swayed. Both Asteria

and Leto were immediately
by my side, Pallas moving forward
to wrap his arm around my waist
to steady me.

'Perhaps . . .' Pallas suggested gently,
'you should rest for a while.'
I shook my head, but leaned into
the solid warmth of his body.

'I will rest when I see her.'
I would rest when I apologized
to her for hiding her true origin
was what I truly wanted to say.

I saw Pallas's jaw tighten slightly.
I could see the conflict in his eyes,
but he nodded.
Perses took this as his signal.

He reached into his bag
and pulled out a fistful of white sand,
which he threw into the sky.
In moments, a hum resounded

and a warm breeze blew around us.
For a moment, I thought
I would have to suffer Zephyrus again.
Instead, a tall, quiet being appeared.

A Goddess.
Her features were striking,
long dark hair flowing to her waist,
dark-bright eyes shining.

I frowned. I thought the Anemoi
were four brothers. But of course,
the one spoken of the least
was the most beautiful, tolerable one.

A sister. A Goddess.
She was Eurus.
The warm desert east wind.
Upon her face were markings

of ancient prayers.
She looked upon us
and asked quietly,
'Where do you wish to go?'

'Aigaion'

It was me who whispered this.
I could not understand why Metis
would be collecting such ingredients
or why she would choose to go to Aigaion.
No God or mortal lived there.

Eurus placed her hands
to each corner of her mouth,
and gave out a lyrical songlike cry.
A smooth, warm carpet of wind
rose under our feet.

Of all four of the Anemoi,
this journey was the only one that
was full of comfort for me
in my condition.
Eurus flicked her wrists

to bring us all easily to the mountain
where Nyx said Metis had gone.
My heart pounded in my chest.
My mind wondering,
what was on Aigaion?

'Styx, How Long Have You Known?'

Pallas appeared by my side as we travelled,
the waters of the ocean shining below
as Hyperion won the day again.

I turned to look at my consort's face,
his handsome features shadowed
with concern and sadness.

'Some time,' I admitted softly.
Then I reached for his hand. 'I did not
want you to stop me from coming.'

He looked down at where my fingers
were entwined with his, then up at me.
'I am not your father, Styx,'

he reminded me gently.
'I have only ever shown you
love and grace. Do you still

not trust me?' At these words,
it was as though a veil fell
from my eyes. I had hurt him.

Not because I kept the baby a secret,
but because I had disrespected his love
in doing so. Even now, Pallas did not

show any anger. Instead,
he simply showed pain.
'Pallas,' I said ruefully.

My heart had been barricaded so long
that I did not recognize his love
for the gift that it was.

And now I had hurt him. The only
male God who had shown me
unconditional understanding and support.

Where my father knew my intelligence
and used it to his benefit without gratitude,
Pallas always thanked me for my counsel.

Where my brothers knew I was eldest
but showed me no respect for it,
Pallas never forgot, mentioning

to anyone who would listen
that I was the first of our generation,
the oldest of the Titans' children.

How had I not seen his patient love
for what it was? Relegated him to being
just another male God unconsciously.

I took his face in my hands and said words
I had rarely ever said before.
'I am sorry. Forgive me, my love.'

Something shifted in his expression.
A relief shone in his eyes.

'You Are Forgiven a Thousand Times Over'

His words warmed and soothed my cold heart.
I had become so used to protecting myself
that I only trusted Asteria completely.

But Pallas, Pallas had been there all along.
I was about to answer him as he pressed
his lips to the inside of my wrist,

when Eurus's husky voice resounded,
'Aigaion.' And gently,
she led the breeze that carried us

all the way down to the mountaintop.
This mountain was in Crete, which knew
warmth better than cold, but the peak

remained snowy throughout the year.
Somewhere on these ranges,
there must be other immortals.

Perhaps Metis knew of this but had
kept it to herself all these years.
A sharp pang of sadness resonated

through my very bones as we
stood on the mountaintop.
Eurus watched us with a hawk's eye.

'Is this not where you needed
to be?' How could we explain it was,
but we did not know

where to look.
I saw amusement cross Eurus's face
the corners of her mouth lifting

in an almost smile. 'Do you need
more aid?' she asked, her voice
not unkind. Asteria answered for us,

knowing Perses and I were too proud,
and Pallas and Leto too tender
to ask for help even when they needed it.

'Please, Eurus. We are looking for Metis.
How does one track a Goddess through
these mountains?' Eurus smiled

'Let me send my winds to fetch
an answer from the trees.'
She snapped her fingers

and the sound of the winds rising
and rustling could be heard
echoing across the mountain peaks.

A hollow sound and then a whistle.
Eurus listened carefully.
'The oaks tell me that a Goddess is here.

She is inside a cavern not far away.'
She paused and her brow furrowed.
Fear wrapped its cold fingers around my heart.

'But You Must Be Cautious. She Is Not Alone.'

The ichor in my veins
turned to ice as she murmured
those words. Of all the Anemoi,
she was the one whom I felt most sure of.

I glanced at the other immortals.
They too held the same concern
in their eyes. Metis was in danger.
Someone or something must have taken her.

On her quest to find ingredients,
someone may have stolen her.
An outrage burst through me.
Who had the audacity to trap a Goddess?

Who had thought they could get away
with such a sacrilegious, vile deed?
My hands balled into fists.
'We need to find her. Now.'

Eurus pointed and said,
'She is in a cavern three mountains
away from here. It is the only cavern
upon that mountain.'

She contemplated something,
then looked at us carefully.
'I wish you good fortune.
And safety.'

The Mouth of the Unknown

I was immortal enough to rarely feel pain,
but there was discomfort in walking
mountain ranges with a baby within my womb.

Asteria and Pallas both helped me
where they could, often exchanging worried
glances. We were headed into the belly

of an unknown beast and I was now so swollen,
it was clear I had a child within me.
A child destined to complete a prophecy.

Just before nightfall we reached the cavern.
This was nothing like Asteria's and my own
hiding place, which was comforting and familiar.

The uneven mouth of this hollow gave me shivers
for what lay within it. The darkness sang
with a cruelty I could not yet name.

I looked to the other immortals with trepidation.
'How do we rescue her if she is trapped?'
asked Leto softly, worry in her gentle eyes.

'Then we will undo the trap,' Perses said.
'If anything stands in our way, I will
destroy it.' Pallas cleared his throat.

'*We* will destroy it.' I was too tired to argue,
knowing that what had taken her was immortal too,
and we had very little chance of their destruction.

Asteria and I held each other's hands tight
and then the five of us began to descend
into the cave.

Hollowed Mountain

It was as though the whole mountain
was carved out on the inside.
The caves descended downward
forever. But we could tell
someone had certainly been here.

Torches hung across the uneven walls
shone the way for us
through the darkness.
A thought occurred to me.
If something malevolent is present,

how would I protect my child?
I laid a hand on my stomach
and felt the life inside me move.
The answer came to me.
You have always known how to fight.

Just when I began to think
that we had been descending
for too long and that maybe
Eurus's oaken spies were wrong,
we heard it. A loud crack.

And then the sound of Metis's laughter.

Metis's Secret

My heart raced with joy,
then excitement, then relief. But before
I could go to her, Pallas grasped my hand.

We quickly hid from view.
We were in the very heart of the mountain,
which opened up into a cavernous space.

It was a thing of wonder,
a strange mirror of my father's banquet hall.
My heartbeat quickened looking at it.

So large that it made us all feel small.
So vast that it held space enough
for all the Gods we knew.

How the mountain stayed upright
when the inside was so hollow
was a strange metaphysical secret.

As we stood, hidden from view
above this gigantic fissure,
we saw her.

Metis, standing in the middle
of the mountain.
And there, by her side,

holding bolts of fire in his hand
was the God from my dark dream.
The one who had destroyed my father's

entire palace with a single hand.

Asteria

A GODDESS OF ORACLES AND FALLING STARS

PART VI

The Voices in My Mind

were slowly building to a crescendo.
A collective scream was coming;
I could feel it and I clutched
Styx's hand tighter.

Calm yourselves, I said to the voices,
I cannot hear what you are saying.
They knew when they spoke
one above the other,

their words were no different
to me than the calls of angry crows.
But looking at Metis
and the strange God at her side,

I could understand what they were saying.
Danger lurked in every corner here.
And something was deeply,
catastrophically wrong.

A Reflection on Metis

I had seen it in her as a child.
The capacity for a deep rage.
The first time was when
she had just started walking.

We had been sitting
on the sandy shores
outside my father's palace.
An albatross dared to steal

the piece of apple
from her clenched fingers.
In moments, this mighty bird
was flung back, as though

it was little more than
a feather, thrown into the ocean
with such power and fury
that I almost did not see it.

The way her eyes had turned
from yellow to fire.
The way her little clenched fist
held a smattering of feathers.

The second time was when
a River God had dared
to chase Leto to the point of fear
all the way from Oceanus's palace

to the threshold of
my father's palace.
Metis had sprung at him
like a cat waiting for prey.

When Leto and I pulled
her off him, he was screaming
in pain, long gold claw marks
across his chest.

Metis had threatened him
into silence. Promised him
worse if he ever told.
I should have known

there was an untamed violence,
a self-preservation within her bones,
like the rivers and oceans
she was born from.

It had been foolish of us
to think that such a secret,
when it came to light,
that her origin story

would not turn her
against us all.

Styx's Face

While we were watching Metis,
trying to determine what she was doing,
who this strange God was,
Styx could not take her eyes off him.
Her split eyes were wide,
her mouth open in fear.

She knew him.
I reached out to take her hand,
finding it even more ice cold
than usual. She turned to me,
barely able to find words,
the hiss in her voice more pronounced.

'It is him, Asteria,' she whispered,
her words trembled as they landed,
making their mark in my own fear.
'He is the one from my dream.
The God who will
destroy us all.'

I Looked Down at Metis and This Strange God

His long silver hair shone
and his body moved
with an elegant lethality.

Something about him made me shiver.
A voice in my head whispered,
Harbinger of Chaos.

I tried to focus despite it. Dismiss it
the way a new oracle would dismiss
a prophetic warning as it was far too bleak.

The silver-haired God
swept Metis up in his arms,
and put his lips upon hers.

He then declared, his voice boisterous,
'When I am king of the Gods,
I shall make you a golden throne

made from the blood of the old Gods.
Together, we shall watch them
beg, and plead, and burn.'

I felt a chill settle on my immortal heart
as Metis smiled at his words,
kissing him in return.

'Zeus. King of the Gods.
Your name will be known across Chaos.'

Zeus

The voices within my head
became even louder.
More and more joined in,
like a chorus of angry shouts.

I winced. It felt like a thousand souls
were imprisoned inside my skull,
dying to get out. Through the noise, they told me
who he was. I clutched Styx's hand.

'H-he is the son of Kronos,'
I whispered, swaying slightly
from the weight of these voices.
Perses moved to my side,

his hand sliding around my waist,
holding me up against his chest.
'He is the son of Kronos,'
I said more clearly so Pallas

and Leto could hear too.
'That is impossible,' Perses said.
'Kronos eats every single child
born to Rhea. Why would he

let a son live, knowing the prophecy?'
The voices in my head screamed
and then suddenly went silent.
I turned to my consort quietly.

A slow harrowing settling
inside my immortal body.
The truth fell out into the darkness.
'Kronos does not know.'

Our Unending Curse

Sometimes, I believe we were always cursed. Chaos ensured it when Ouranos usurped Gaia to become our king. I do not think the great creator of us all ever wanted us to have a king or even a queen. The reason Gaia originally ruled was because we turned to her rivers, her forests, her soil for aid. We built our palaces on her gifts. Her abundance flowed through our own veins. Perhaps the darkening of Ouranos's soul came when he saw how much we depended on Gaia. He saw her position as queen, while we simply saw her as mother. When he forced the Hecatoncheires – those hundred-handed, fifty-headed siblings of the golden Titans – back into Gaia's womb as he determined them too ugly to exist, he forced her into an isolation due to pain. And in that time, he ruled instead of fathered us. He took instead of gave. In some ways, when Gaia gave Kronos the sickle that cleaved him, it was out of mercy. In other ways, it was vengeance. But when he was overthrown and cleaved, he wrote our prophecy in stone in golden blood: *'Your son will destroy you, just as you have destroyed me. Your reign, oh Kronos, will not last long.'* In a way, madness was the only answer. In a way, what other choice did Kronos have once he was cursed?

Metis and Zeus

were not paying attention.
If they were, they would have heard
Styx's gasp, her heavy breathing,
our worried low voices
asking what was wrong.

When I turned back to check
where Metis and Zeus were,
I saw they were still wrapped up
in each other's arms,
Metis telling him,

'I have finished the spell.
The stone is ready for you.'
From a bag on her hip,
she removed what looked like
a glowing crimson-and-gold ruby,

so large she needed two hands to hold it.
Zeus took it from her,
his eyes glinting with bloodlust,
raising it to the light to see it.
'And no one is any the wiser?'

'None of the old Gods asked any questions
and when Nyx did, I told her
it was a matter of fate.'
A shudder coursed through my body.
When had Metis become so good
at this game of lies?

Perhaps it was my father's mistake.

It was he who made her
the Goddess of Wisdom and Cunning.
He thought she would turn out like him,
the God of Intellect, with such gifts.
Instead . . . she was a Goddess of Endings.

Instead, she had become the reason
that everything we knew might fall.
Zeus kissed her lips again.
'You are magnificent.
This is why you shall be my queen.'

I watched Metis run her finger
along his jawline. 'It is time for you
to go practise thunder and lightning.
Nyx has taken the sky.
Your father will be asleep.'

Zeus gave her the red-gold stone.
And after she put it into her bag,
he lifted her hands to his face
to kiss them. 'I shall return at dawn.'
All of us breathed a sigh of relief

as we watched him walk to the other side
of the cave and leave.

Styx's Hand Grew Tighter on Mine

At first, I thought it was only fear,
but when I turned to her, I knew.

I knew from when we had helped
Tethys birth Metis that day long ago.

The child was coming.
Goddesses give birth at whim.

Great swells of emotion sometimes
cause a child to be born before its time.

I should have taken Styx from this cave
as soon as we saw Metis with Zeus.

And now, she clutched my hand,
trying so hard not to cry out.

Pallas moved to support her quickly
and we helped her onto the floor.

For a moment, other than
her laboured breathing,

there was a silence that made us
assume we were safe.

We assumed too soon.

Styx's Cry Pierced the Air

and it was as though the whole world
began to eclipse slowly.
I turned my head to see Metis
look up in the direction of the cry.

Metis's eyes met mine.
Yellow and cold at first,
but then recognition as her gaze
widened to panic and she ran.

She ran toward us but Perses
stood and blocked her path.
I did not want to leave Styx's hand
as she cried out louder.

She had always said she was afraid
of bringing a God child into this world.
But as Perses blocked Metis from us,
his large, muscular body in her way,

I had to let Styx's hand go
and grasp his shoulder.
'She is our sister,' I said fiercely.
'She will not hurt Styx. Let her pass.'

Perses hesitated,
but saw the fire in my eyes.
Without another word,
he let Metis join us.

The First Birth

Styx had never wanted children.
She had told me that if she had been
a Goddess, she would have had a choice.

It was true there were those among us
who did not choose to be consorts.
But it was a rare thing for even a Goddess

not to choose to have a child.
Kneeling, I took Styx's hand again.
Metis sat between her legs.

'Perses,' I spoke urgently,
'bring us water, clean cloths.'
Metis looked at me and shook her head.

'There is no need,' she snapped her fingers,
and suddenly, there was a large golden bowl
full of water beside us, and swaddling cloths.

My jaw tightened.
Clearly Metis was further along
than both Styx and I in her powers.

Why did she not tell us any of this?
But there was no time to think,
as Styx began to push.

I pressed a cool, wet cloth to her forehead.
Her cries filled the cave. The process
of birth took time and strength.

While Pallas held Styx's other hand,
whispering soothing words to her,
Perses kept careful watch for Zeus.

I was grateful for his distraction.
But I was afraid our own children
might have to be born this way.

Not in a palace, a safe home of Gods,
but in some cave hidden far away.
As hours passed and Styx bravely

bore the agonizing pain,
never complaining through her
suffering, finally the cries of an infant

filled all the many corners of the cave.
It occurred to me in that moment
how far we had come from our own girlhood.

And how fitting it was in some ways
that it was in a cave much like our
beloved one from childhood that

Styx had given birth to the first child
from amongst the four of us.
Metis swaddled and held the infant.

'It is a boy,' she whispered softly,
reverently, and placed him on Styx's chest.

Pallas's Amber Eyes Shone

so bright, they looked like the sun.
I realized I had never seen him shed tears.

Most Gods did not. They saw
tears and grief as the actions

of lesser deities, Goddesses, and mortals.
But Pallas in that moment could not have been

more powerful than when he placed
his hand on his son's small head,

his other holding Styx's hand tight,
a slight tremble in his fingers.

'A child of zeal.' His voice deepened.
'A God of dedication and emulation.

Rivals will pray to him. He will inspire
the competition and envy of the world.'

They were fearsome and powerful gifts.
And it was clear that this child in temperament

would be more like his mother than his father.
Styx had finally caught her breath,

her face still covered in a sheen
of holy perspiration, the exertion

of childbirth having not left her easily.
She clutched the baby to her chest,

her split eyes full of something
I never thought I would see in her:

pure, unadulterated love. Gone was her spite,
her grief, her sadness. I asked

the question we all wanted to:
'What is the child's name?'

Styx looked up at Pallas as she answered,
squeezing his hand tight.

'His name is Zelus. Our child made
of zeal and surprise.'

The Baby's Cries Soothed

and after some time had passed,
Styx sat up with help from Pallas,

her divine body healing quickly.
As she rocked the child at her chest,

she looked up at Metis.
But it was I who spoke first to her.

'Metis,' I sighed, 'why?'
Metis, who had been in silent awe

watching Styx with Zelus,
slowly turned toward me.

Her eyes were narrow,
anger written in the corners of her mouth.

'*Why?* You dare to ask *me* why?
You have all been lying to me.'

Her hands shook. 'You knew.
You knew and you called yourself

my sisters.' Leto stepped forward
to take Metis's hand but she wrenched

it away. 'And you, Leto.' Her voice rose.
'I thought you were my ally, my friend.'

Leto's eyes filled with tears.
'I am, Metis. We did it to protect you!

Who knows what Kronos would have done
if he had learned a new Oceanid had—'

Metis threw her head back
and let out a short, bitter laugh.

'Kronos does not scare me.
And he should not scare you either.'

It was Styx who spoke now.
She rose from where she lay,

handing Zelus tenderly to Pallas.
'Metis, I understand your pain.

I understand being betrayed by your own.
Please know that we were only trying

to protect you from the rage of the God-King.'
Metis faltered, but her eyes hardened again.

'That is why the God-King must fall.
A God-King should be fair, not cruel.'

Perses stepped forward now.
'And what makes you think,'

he said quietly, his voice cold,
'that Zeus would be any better?'

Metis's Eyes Burned with Fire

'Zeus was brought up by Goddesses.
By his mother, Rhea, as an infant,
the mountain nymph Adrastia as a child,
and now, it is I who brought him
into his godhood. We have trained him
well to be everything his father is not.'

Perses shook his head.
'Power does not work this way, Metis.
Do you not understand what storm
you are about to unleash?'
I put my hand on my consort's shoulder.
Upsetting her would make things worse.

Styx pleaded, her voice softer than
I had ever heard it. 'My dear one.
The amount of times I have wanted
to give you the truth. All this time
I wanted to tell you. You must know,
no one here wanted to hurt you.

We have always loved you.
Have we ever given you a reason
to doubt our love?'
At these words, Metis was silent.
And then, her face growing weary,
she sighed deeply.

'No. I have never had cause to doubt your love.
That is why this hurt. And Rhea was . . .'
She squared her shoulders and stood tall,
'Rhea needed help. Support. Zeus was close to
my age when she asked me to aid her.
She could not manage his powers alone.

He was far too powerful for his own good
and he needed someone to guide him.
Who better than the Goddess of Wisdom
and Cunning? Ask yourself
what you would do if your children
were devoured by their own fathers?

Ask yourself what you would do
if you lived with a mad king?
Would you not try to save
your own children too?
Would you not pay any price?'
She took a deep breath.

'And if a Goddess came to you
and begged you to help her protect
a child you knew was in danger,
your own kin, would you not
do everything in your power
to save that child too?'

Her Words Rang True

Especially in this moment,
where one of us held
a newborn child
in their arms.

Metis looked at each
of our faces.
'How can you blame me,'
she whispered,

'for doing what each of you
would have done?'
I couldn't help it.
I reached out

and took her hand.
'Metis,' I gently spoke,
'I understand you wished
to help Rhea.

But have you
considered
what will happen
if Kronos falls?'

Metis sighed deeply
and closed her eyes
as she thought.
A collective silence descended.

When she opened her eyes
she said, 'Let me speak
to Zeus. He listens
to my counsel.'

The sound of thunder
from above woke Zelus
and his cries resounded
inside the cave.

Metis took my hand
and Styx's hand.
'You must go, quickly,
before he returns.'

We nodded at her,
but something in her voice
gave me pause.
Was she afraid of Zeus?

The truth was a broken thing
shining between us all
inside the darkness.
A glowing orb that said,

No matter what happens,
everything has changed.
And nothing can be hidden.
Not now or ever again.

Eurus Was Waiting

High on the mountaintop
she sat, playing a flute,
a whistling song
that the wind danced to.

When she saw us climbing
toward her, she stopped.
She reached down to help Styx
and smiled at Zelus in Pallas's arms

'A new little one,' she breathed.
'He is beautiful.'
Zelus, his eyes blown open,
grasped Eurus's finger

as she caressed his soft cheek.
Amber-eyed like his father,
and green-haired like his mother,
he was already alert to the world.

'Where do you wish to go?'
Eurus asked us.
None of us spoke for some time.
In the end it was Perses who answered,

'Oceanus's palace.'
I looked at him,
his mouth was set
in a grim line.

'We should go to my father's home,'
I told him, my voice soft
but determined.
'No,' Perses disagreed.

'We must warn Oceanus.'
I considered Metis,
her role in all this.
Her promise to us.

'Give Metis time to speak to Zeus,'
I said, and Styx and Leto agreed.
'If you tell Oceanus now,
he will react poorly

and it is Metis who will pay
the ultimate price for this.'
Perses did not answer,
and with a jolt, I realized

he believed Metis
should be punished
for her actions here.
But he did not say it.

Looking at my face,
he softened and acquiesced.
'We will give her time.
But once we hear from her,

we must do what is right
by our own kind.
The older Titans must know
of the storm coming toward us all.'

It Took the Life Cycle of a Day and Night

but Eurus carried us home.
The warm breeze kept Zelus comfortable
and Styx fed him with care.
It was strange to watch her
with a child now.

Perses squeezed my hand gently.
'One day we will have one of our own.'
I smiled at his words, but truthfully,
given the precarity of our lives,
since the discovery of Zeus,

I was unsure I wanted to bring
a Titan child into a world
where Titans were being threatened.
But this was what was expected of us,
Goddesses and nymphs alike.

To create more deities like our consorts,
to give them children
with powers and eternities.
For Gods and mortal men alike,
progeny were their legacy.

For Goddesses and women,
children meant a lifetime
of care, nurture, giving.
The only one who did not participate
in this ritual it seemed,

despite her many, many children,
was Nyx. But then,
Nyx was also the Goddess

feared by every God
who ever existed.

When we arrived
at my father's palace,
a strange kind of melancholy
took over my very bones.
My heart throbbed with a dull ache.

Something told me to treasure
these moments well.
So I let Perses take me
by the hand and say,
'My father and I built

a palace long ago,
where I would bring my own consort to.
Instead of remaining here,
would you like to go
there instead?'

I should have refused.
But his amber eyes sparkled
and my desire for him
grew the closer he stepped.
I smiled and breathed,

'Yes, take me home.'

Our New Home

To say it was beautiful would be a disservice to this place of dreams that Perses had created with his father's help. It sat on an island not far from my own father's palace, a bright marble structure that was full of open courtyards. Fountains of water drew in birds from across the world, the courtyards were home to peacocks and parakeets alike, white snowy owls lived in its tall marble towers. And behind the palace was a wilderness, its own forest of flora and fauna, wild hare and deer roaming free. But it was the largest courtyard that Perses took me to, one behind the palace, still enclosed safely behind its marble walls, but with enough space for three temples if not more. He told me this was mine to turn into a garden of my very own. A place where I could grow all the herbs and flowers I'd like. He told me he would build me an altar so that I could send the smoke to my Oracles, grant their prophecies. And the highest tower, he promised me would be turned into a place where I could see the stars and help them fall – showing them the way as I always did. It was only then that he took me to our own chambers hidden away within the heart of this fine palace, its airy hallways and arches, its bright courtyards full of colourful birds, and its secret forests and fountains, all welcoming me home.

The Dream

Five nights passed and I should have been
in the most peaceful rest of my immortality.

Instead, as Perses slept beside me,
I fell into a troubled, strange sleep.

My body tensed with a certain fear,
something I could not name.

I was not surprised at the red sky
of my dream, the sign of warnings.

But what made my heart
beat like a drum within my chest

was from the red sky above,
I heard the cries of a thousand Gods.

The sound of adamantine clashing
against adamantine,

and loudest of all, I heard the sound
of thunder. Thunder that raged

as I watched ichor fall
like fire from the sky

into the churning seas below.

Perses Called for Me

At first, I thought it was part of my dream.
His voice was frayed with unease.
The way he said my name darkened
with an urgency I could not place.

My body went rigid as I felt huge hands
on my shoulders, shaking me awake,
and it was then that I realized,
this was not part of my prophetic dream.

My eyes flew open and I gazed
into Perses's golden eyes,
wild with concern,
while mine were wild with confusion.

'Perses?' I asked, sitting up.
Outside Eos was bringing in the dawn,
her rosy fingers painting the sky.
My consort took a deep breath.

'Asteria, we have received an urgent
summons. All the Gods and deities
have been called to Oceanus's palace.
We must leave at once, my love.'

Only a few nights had passed
since our return. My heart raced
in my chest. This was disquieting.
Had Metis failed to convince Zeus?

The Universal Summons

When we arrived at Oceanus's palace,
its high arches and marble floors
that I had once known so well
felt unwelcoming and strange.

The air was stifling as we made
our way to the halls where
a thousand great feasts for immortals
of every kind were held.

Perses pushed opened the heavy doors
and took my hand as he led me in.
A magnificent yet terrifying sight
awaited us within this place.

I did not know it was possible
to fit so many powerful Gods
into these halls, which seemed
even larger than I remembered them.

The lesser deities positioned themselves
near the door, River Gods
and nymphs alike jostling
to take up as much space

as they possibly could.
Beyond them were
the more powerful
children of the Titans.

Styx and Pallas were amongst them
as well as Leto. Metis was nowhere to be seen.
Perses and I went to take our place
by their side, our faces grim.

Next to the children of Titans
stood ten of the twelve children
of Gaia and Ouranos, the old Titans
and Titanides themselves.

Beyond them on thrones
made of silver and gold,
sat the most ancient of us all.
The five Primordials.

Even Tartarus had left his volcano.
I glanced at Styx and saw she shared
my great unease. Zelus was at Pallas's
chest, already grown into a child.

We grew silent.
It was Oceanus who spoke
in the quiet that followed.
'Primordials. Titans. Children

of Gods and immortals.
You have been summoned here
on the askance of your elders
as a certain darkness shadows our horizon.'

At his words, the sound of thunder
roared across the skies beyond.

A Hush Fell Over All the Deities Assembled

It felt as though an era passed
before Oceanus continued,
his voice as dark as an oncoming storm.

'We have received word that Kronos,
our God-King, is under attack.'
A gasp rose from all of us.

I turned to Styx, my heart clenched.
Our eyes connected and we knew:
Metis had failed to stop Zeus.

As we had since we were girls,
we reached for each other's hands.
I clasped her cold fingers tight,

trying to soothe us both
as fear coursed through us.
Oceanus took a deep breath.

'For an age now, we have all been
visited by many prophecies,
blessings from Chaos herself.

It is now time for us to face
what these prophecies mean.
Kronos's rule has been challenged.'

But before he could say more,
the large, heavy doors swung open.

With a Crackle of Blinding Light

Zeus stepped into the hall.
Behind him were five strangers.

Each one was bright and gleaming
silver unlike the golden Titans.

Even from here, I could feel their rage;
I could feel their sheer power.

Zeus made his way to the thrones,
the five strange Gods following behind him.

Oceanus scowled, his voice rising.
'Who enters my home without permission?'

Zeus had a smirk on his bearded face
as he responded to this with hubris.

'The children of Kronos, Titan.
The same ones you left to be devoured.'

A shocked murmur swept across the deities.
Zeus raised his voice, thunder roaring.

'Did you think you would not have to atone
for abandoning us within the darkness?'

From the Corner of My Eye

I saw Perses's fists clench.
I saw Pallas hold Zelus close,
the boy clutching his robes.
A palpable fear hung in the air.

Leto took my other hand,
and as I looked into her eyes
I saw it there, the mirror of my thoughts.
We should have told them.

We should not have left
such a task to Metis alone.
She may have failed us,
but we had failed her first.

Oceanus finally spoke out loud.
'Your father's choices as king
were not our choices to make.'
A raven-haired Goddess amongst

Zeus's siblings let out a bitter laugh.
'You would have left us to rot
in his stomach for eternity. You had
choices. You chose our suffering.'

Zeus put his hand on her shoulder
to calm her.
He then turned back to Oceanus.
'As this was your choice, mighty Titans,

we decree you incapable
of reigning over the realms.
We decree you unable to rule
with the nobility and dignity

required of great leaders.'
It was as though the very hall
had darkened to the threat
of an endless abyss.

It was my father, thus far holding back,
who stepped forward, his eyes
a hurricane of anger.
He shouted, 'Insolent children!

You have no right to decree
anything. You have no say here.
You are in the house of Titans
and we do not bow to strangers.'

I had never seen him so enraged,
never known Coeus the Calm
to hold such fury in his voice.
It was in that moment I felt it.

The full scale of what was to come.
Our world was about to change,
and how the old Titans handled
what came next would define

our entire future.

It Was Gaia Who Spoke

Our grandmother, with her forest hair
and her tired eyes, looked upon us and said,

'Children and grandchildren,
this quarrel is misplaced.

As the oldest of you, we too
had to make room for the new Gods.

We handed so much of the realms
to our children as the next generation.

It is the duty of the old to make way for the new.
This is the greatest lesson you will ever learn.

Let go of your hubris
and allow new blood to rule.'

While her words were wise and keen
in her strategy to avoid conflict,

I could see that neither the Titans nor Zeus
and his brothers and sisters seemed

appeased in any way.

Gentle Atlas Raised His Voice Next

'Child of Kronos, taking out the sins of
your father on the rest of divinity is the act
of a small and brutal immortal.'

Atlas's voice was soft but with a hidden edge.
'If you declare us unworthy of our realms,
what makes you believe *you* are worthy?'

Zeus placed a hand inside the bag
by his side and raised a glowing orb,
the orb Metis had made.

'None of you had the courage to do this.
To force this down my father's gullet.
To release my brothers and sisters

as they lay hostage within him.
None of you had the courage to face him.'
He threw the orb to the ground triumphantly.

'Unlike you, I do not leave Gods to suffer.
I do not leave my kin to languish
in an eternity they do not deserve.'

He raised his head high. 'Accept
that we are your new rulers;
I am your new God-King.'

Atlas's cold voice held a challenge.
'Or?'

'Or Perish'

The words were uttered with such icy fury
that the voices in my head began to clamour.

Zeus did not intend for this to be resolved
with any kind of conciliation.

He and his siblings had come here
with a singular notion.

That was to control
the realms of the Titans.

And if we did not give them up willingly,
they would take them by force.

Styx held my hand tighter as Oceanus spoke.
'Gods do not perish, child.'

Zeus smiled at him. 'But Gods can be punished.
They can be trapped inside darkness.

They can be hurt. Their wives and daughters
can be enslaved. Is that the fate

you choose for yourselves and your families?'
The ten Titans were completely silent.

My ichor turned to ice inside my body
as I heard my father finally say the words,

'If it is a battle you want, child,
then it is a battle you will get.'

Zeus Turned to Us at This

'Do you hear that, children of Titans?
Your fathers have abandoned you.
Given the choice of peace and bloodshed,
they have chosen to sacrifice you.

I am a kinder ruler. Any Titan who joins me
will be allowed to keep some of their powers
and pieces of their realms. They will win favour
with me and no harm will come to them.'

None of us moved. Zeus continued to speak,
his voice cold and unwavering.
'And those of you who have never tasted power
in this Titan hierarchy will finally know godhood.

I will give this choice, this offer to you.'
With these words, Zeus and his siblings
departed the palace of Oceanus, leaving behind
a bitter taste of poisoned air in their wake.

We Who Had Never Known War

No Primordial had fought for Ouranos.
No one had raised their voice in his favour
or held court for him or declared against Gaia

or Kronos or his Titan siblings.
Instead the Primordials had taken refuge
within their own realms, leaving the rest

of the realms to the Titans to rule.
If they wanted, they could have crushed
Gaia's golden children. Instead, they did

what Gaia had now asked her own children to do.
Let go of the old. Make room for the new.
So Zeus's decree had shaken us all to the core.
What would we do now?

A Visitor

Hyperion's sun was nowhere
when the five of us left the palace.
Storm clouds had turned the whole sky grey.

The sea was an ink blue,
its fathomless depths
threatening a hurricane.

The bright sands we knew
as children were an ash white,
the whole world leached of colour.

Just as Perses turned to say
something, I saw a figure
walking toward us.

Against the white sands,
their dark shroud stood out.
The stranger arrived before us;

the shroud fell to their shoulders.
It was her.

Metis's Return

Her eyes lowered, she said softly,
'I tried to stop him. But he has
his own destiny to fulfil.'

My hands shook as I took hers.
'Please do not blame yourself.
His rage is an unstoppable force.

And anger like that cannot be sated
with kindness and wise words.'
I left the rest unspoken.

We knew his rage was driven
by vengeance. A vengeance rooted
in betrayal was hard to quench.

It could not be fed ambrosia,
only ichor. Styx's voice was hushed,
her face even paler than before.

'We failed you, Metis.
We should have understood
where this would lead.

In our quest to protect you,
we did to you what I hated
being done to me.

We kept secrets. Now . . .'
She swallowed hard.
'Now we all must pay the price.'

Metis's eyes filled with tears.
'You must understand,
Zeus is not a terrible God.

He has been raised with
a singular purpose.
Rhea poured all her unspoken

sadness and fury into him.
What choice did he have
other than to become this?'

Perses interrupted.
'He could choose not to
destroy his kin who have not

harmed him, Metis.'
I stared at him. His voice
was so callous. I had never

heard him speak this way before
to anyone. I stepped
between him and Metis.

'Perhaps,' I said, 'the lesson
here is that we should all
see injustice for what it is,

so no more Titan children
thirst for revenge.'
Perses let out a bitter laugh.

'Do you not understand still?'
His golden eyes seemed frigid.
'It is too late. If Zeus has his way

there will be no Titans left.'
Metis shook her head vehemently.
'He would not do that.'

Pallas, still holding Zelus close,
looked at Metis with kindness and pity.
'That is what he told us today.

And do you not remember
him promising you a throne
made from Titan blood?'

Styx put her arm around Metis.
'Come with us,' she pleaded.
'Come and tell our father all you know.'

Metis seemed torn.
But then she moved away from Styx.
'I cannot. I have already pledged

my allegiance to Zeus
and Kronos's children.'
What was our sister saying?

I felt like my heart was collapsing.
'Metis,' I whispered,
'you are saying you are against us?'

She stared at us, yellow eyes strange
and distant. 'Zeus is my consort.
I cannot turn against him.'

A Terrible Revelation

Styx's eyes widened and she stepped back.
My own heart felt so heavy, as though
it contained the entire weight of the sea.

'You have already had the ceremony?'
I asked her, my voice raw with pain.
She was staring at us still with that distant gaze.

'I am carrying his child,' she said simply.
'And I am to be his queen of Gods.
I will rule beside him.'

The silence that followed her words
filled me with fear. Metis was impassive.
Styx stared at her and her eyes narrowed.

'Metis,' she hissed, 'he does not even
have a realm of his own yet. Rule where?'
Our sister's face broke into a smile that sent

shudders down my spine. 'The children
of Kronos have chosen Olympus as their home.
They no longer wish to be called Titans.

They are called the Olympians.'
She looked at me and took my hand gently.
'You could all join us.' She turned to Styx.

'We could use your might
in the coming storm.'

'Never'

Sword-edged, the word was said quietly
by Perses, but it made its mark.

Metis straightened to her full height.
'You can choose to stay with those lying

old Gods who have treated us all with such
callousness, as though we did not matter.'

She looked at Styx. 'Who reduced your status
from what should have been Goddess to nymph.'

She glanced at Leto and me. 'Who made you
keep terrible secrets to protect themselves.'

She smiled again, this time colder.
'Or you could choose the winning side.'

Perses's body went rigid next to mine.
'I will never betray my family, Metis.'

The implication hung within the air.
Metis sighed with a finality.

'Very well.' Her voice was a whisper.
'Goodbye then, my sisters.'

Her eyes closed.
And then she was gone.

It All Happened Suddenly

No sooner had we returned to our palace
than Perses was summoned to the halls
of Hyperion. He was told by the Titans
that the threat from Zeus needed a response.

That it would be his duty to devise
this counterattack. Pallas was told
his role would be to make weaponry
for the Titan Gods who stood against Zeus.

During this time, every Titan God
was to stay at Kronos's palace
while they created this strategy.
Every Titanide, nymph, and Goddess

was meant to look after the new
brood of Titan children throughout this,
but our movements were limited
in case a surprise attack was launched

onto our homes by these unpredictable
Olympians. A golden cage for golden Gods.
I tried to create harmony
by making a garden of herbs, building my altars,

communicating with my Oracles.
But the prophecies revealed little.
Only the falling of ichor from the skies.
Only the sound of Gods screaming in the night.

The God-King's Decree

Arise now, oh Titans, let no new God tell us ancients what it is to lead our realms. There may be darkness at our footsteps, but we have the house of Hyperion's light by our side. There may be a hurricane at our gates, but the house of Oceanus's Great River stands by us. Rouse your powers, your duty, your honour. May your swords hold true, may your spears find their marks, may Time sing a thousand odes to our courage. Arise, oh sons of Gaia, and protect this earth, its sea and sky that have been ordained only as ours. The wind, the oceans, and all the stars favour us. Victory is ours. Let us take it.

Hubris

Eras into posterity,
mortals will tell stories
about how the Gods hate hubris.
What they will not say
is how it was Zeus
who hated it most.

The Titans had determined
that they would win.
That Zeus and his siblings
were outnumbered.
Victory was already
marked by Titan pride.

When the war first began,
the Titan brothers utilized
every strength they had,
and for an eon, it looked
as though Zeus and his siblings
were easy enough to defeat.

But Zeus was a wily God
and he knew that old deities
would also have old enemies
waiting to be recruited.
He appealed to his grandmother,
Gaia, who sent aid his way.

The Titans did not realize that Zeus
and his siblings were driven
by a vengeance so powerful
it could destroy everything.
Even the most ancient
of Titan Gods.

A War Begins

Each night I would watch Perses return home
long after Nyx had painted the sky dark.

He would bring his weary body to bed,
and I would soothe him in my arms.

'They are stronger than we understood,'
he told me once tiredly.

'Poseidon, he has powerful sway
over water and weapons alike.

Hera is stealthy and controls the birds
who inform her of our every movement.

Hestia seems kind, but her power over
fire can devastate whole forests.

Demeter can rot the world whenever
she wishes and turn it into a corpse.

And Hades. He is enthralled with death;
his hands are made for war and damage.'

After so many evenings of stories like this,
I was not surprised the day the messenger came

and told me Perses would
not return home that night.

Styx

THE RIVER OF THE DEAD

PART VII

My Second Child Was Born as Ichor Fell from the Sky

Whereas my mother's many children
had been born in peace,
some while the sun shone,
others during peaceful nights,
and a few during storms,

my second child was born
into a war. Her father was summoned
to the house of Kronos
where he was told he would build
weaponry for his Titan brothers.

Pallas and I had not yet built
our own palace. And it was
my father's insistence that
all the rest of my children
were born under his watchful eye,

as his prophetic dream
revealed how important they
would be during the war.
The agreement was forged
between Oceanus and Pallas.

No one asked how I felt.
What I had hoped was that Asteria
would invite us to live with her
and Perses. But as days passed,
no such invitation came.

I bitterly realized I had to accept
that my fate was once again
to continue in Oceanus's palace.
But now, I had nowhere to escape to.
I tried to busy myself in the raising

of Zelus, but by the time the Titans
launched their first attack on
those new Gods of Olympus,
he was already a grown God.
And this meant he was taken from me.

I had tried to protest, but what could I say?
He was as mighty as his father and his uncles.
The morning he left to join the conflict,
I had cried so much
my heart never healed.

As I watched him accompany
his father to the house of Kronos,
I feared his capture and injury.
His emerald hair and temperament,
which he inherited from me,

often felt like the only
commonality between us.
Pallas almost missed the birth of Nike,
my child of victory, born on a night
of powerful raging thunder.

Three of my sisters helped me
give birth that night, and I could
feel their hands trembling
as the din rolled across
the skies, blinding lightning

at the windows. The birth
was long and difficult.
It was why I named her Nike.
And it was why I asked Pallas
to give her the gift of victory.

'She will be everything,'
he had decreed, his prophecy
voice shaking with emotion.
'From the good cheer
to the hope we need.'

My sweet rosy-cheeked child
opened her eyes at his words,
as though, even as rumbling rolled
across an uncertain posterity,
she understood what she must do.

I Often Wondered If a Time Before This Existed

That a time where there was peace,
where we didn't hear cries and screams
from the skies, was simply a dream.

Pallas would visit my bed so little now,
his once-bronzed body forever covered
in the soot and charcoal of the forge.

The less I saw him, the more I resented him.
No Goddesses had been called to join the war yet,
and neither had any of us nymphs, of course.

We were relegated to the task of raising progeny,
of keeping the home and hearth safe,
of tending to the wounded.

And there were so many wounded.
The first time I saw my brothers return,
their bodies cut to pieces by adamantine,

some holding their severed legs
in their hands, others holding
their own heads, I wondered

whether immortality was a punishment,
and whether the mortals were more fortunate
for they knew the sweet endless peace of death.

No prophecy or dream could have prepared us
for the unfathomable horror of divine war.

She Appeared One Day from Nowhere

I was resting after the birth of my third child,
Kratos – my child of strength.
He came into this world with a wail so loud
Nike covered her ears
before cleaning and swaddling him.

When she placed Kratos on my chest,
I was startled to see that like me,
he had split eyes. Of all my children,
he was the loudest, the angriest,
and perhaps this was why he looked

the most like me. But where I wore
my rage with a repression,
Kratos embraced his. When
he was taken by his sister and aunts
to meet his grandfather,

I fell back into the comfort
of a deep sleep. Until I heard
the *knock, knock, knock*.
I turned to the balcony,
where the sound was coming from,

and there she stood.
Metis, in all her treacherous
glory. Gone was
her black shroud.
She now wore fine clothes

made of golden silks.
Upon her head was a golden wreath.
And I noticed the sword

by her side, an adamantine
atrocity, large and brutal.

But I knew from her face,
she was not here to harm me.
She would not be so foolish
to come here to hurt me.
For what was I worth?

I was of no true value to this war.
When I gestured for her to enter,
I murmured a quiet spell
to ensure my chamber doors
remained shut so no one entered.

'Metis,' I said coldly.
'Why are you here?'

'I Have Come With an Offer'

Her words made me narrow my eyes.
What could she possibly offer me now?

I watched as she sat down at the edge
of my bed. Her long white hair flowed

to her waist and she looked every part
the ethereal God-Queen

'What is it?' I asked,
in no mood for games or tricks.

'Sister,' she said, 'Zeus meant
what he said when he offered godhood

and clemency in exchange for loyalty.'
I snatched in a deep breath, my heart

suddenly starting to race.
She looked out of the window to lightning clashing.

'We need your support. Already,
Titans are starting to join us.

There is little chance if more take our side
that Zeus will not win this war.'

A Deep Fear Grew Like Ivy Around My Heart

What did this mean for the Titans?
Zeus had made terrible threats
to the Gods who did not take his side,
but cruellest of all were his threats
of what he would do their daughters
and wives – that we would belong
to the Olympian Gods to do
with us what they willed.

But most importantly of all,
what did this mean for my children?
Especially my child of victory, Nike?
I had demanded that Pallas make her
a Goddess so that she could have
protection that I did not.
But could goddesshood protect her
from the lust of more powerful Gods?

'Fear Not, Sister'

Metis's voice was soft and gentle,
but my eye stayed on her sword.
While it was ugly, made with unskilled hands,
I knew the damage adamantine
weapons could do from healing
hundreds of my brothers.

'What are you saying, Metis?'
I asked her quietly, the hiss
hiding the tremor of fear in my own voice.
Outside my door, I heard movement.
I turned to meet her eyes again.
'You must hurry and tell me.'

'I know you have always longed for
goddesshood. To be valued.
And why would you not?
You are the eldest of the Titan children,
and like Asteria and me, you too
are blessed with strange gifts.'

She continued, her voice steady.
'What if I told you that for your loyalty,
Zeus will grant you goddesshood?
He will grant you so many gifts
that your name will be on every
single mortal's lips. Songs
will be sung about you, Styx.'

I took a deep breath,
my whole body turned rigid.
But was this rigidity
fear?
Or was it . . . hope?

Metis's Offer Sang Within My Mind

To go from nymph to Goddess
was all I had ever craved.
To have power over my destiny.
To be more than consort,
more than a vessel for children.

I was the only nymph in my family
of Gods. Pallas and all my children
held powers I could only dream of.
Asteria and I had left our magicking skills behind
the day we went to find Metis.

We had released our creatures
and even given our starfox away.
Wars had no use for my sweet eels,
my small crabs, my gentle starfish.
And why would I attract attention

by focusing on these strange powers
I once had, in the midst of a war.
I finally had a chance to become a Goddess.
But . . . the cost. The cost was
betrayal of everyone I loved.

Betrayal of my father and mother,
my sisters and brothers.
And I knew well enough now
with Perses leading the Titan forces,
he would never turn on his own

and neither would Asteria.
Could I ever do that to her,
my closest friend?

Blinking back tears,
I looked Metis in the eye

and said quietly,
'I cannot do as you have done.
Your price is much too high, Metis.
My answer will have to be no.'
An ache rose in my body as I spoke.

'It Could All Be Yours, Styx'

Metis's gentle coaxing voice
whispered like a viper in my ear.

'Everything you could ever want;
everything you have ever desired.

So close. All you must do is say yes,
and your children and consort

will have Zeus's protection.
You will be a Goddess,

given the respect, the love,
the *fear*, you have always deserved.'

When I did not respond, she sighed.
'I will leave this for you to consider.

Just know that by choosing us,
you are still choosing family.

Know that there are other kin
who have taken this choice.'

Before I could ask who,
Metis rose in all her gold finery,

and with a clever flick of her wrist,
she was gone.

Motherhood

It was unseemly to have even a modicum of joy in this time of deep crisis and agony, and yet . . . motherhood surprised me. It found me holding my children, enjoying their little laughs. Their shouts of discovery inside Oceanus's palace, even with the din of war shaking the glass and leaving thin crevices along the floors. Their quick growth meant I had less time to enjoy their sweet little voices, their unsteady footsteps as they learned how to walk, their claps as I showed them flowers, starfish, other little things that held their attention. I danced with Nike as she listened to my sisters play the flute and I laughed as Kratos learned how to steal my little seashell brush to brush his own hair. I longed for Asteria still. Wished I could show her how lovely my Nike was. Wished I could introduce her to boisterous little Kratos. I wondered often what she would say when she met them. But if I thought of her too long, my heart would ache. A hundred times I thought to write. But I did not know what to say, and we were forbidden from sending messages to each other in case the Olympians read some piece of secret in them that could win them the war. So instead I held my children close. Even now in the middle of all this tragedy and fear, I found little moments of peace with my growing children. Even now in moments of despair, I found little moments of hope.

When Pallas Came Home Many Nights Later

he arrived with harsh news.
'Even with inferior weaponry
the Olympian forces are strong,'
he said bitterly, as I gently
washed his soot-filled hair.

'Zeus's lightning bolts are so powerful
they can crack through adamantine.'
His voice held a tremor I had
never heard before.
'I cannot keep up with the demand.'

I listened to him and replied,
'But our Gods are more numerous.
Surely the sheer strength of numbers
should be enough to destroy them?'
Pallas shook his head.

'A number of Titans have turned.
But we are fortunate your father
has so many children. I am
not sure what we would do
without the Potamoi.'

A cold chill ran through me at his words.
'What about Zelus?'
I asked softly. Pallas turned
to look me in the eye.
'I promise no harm

will come to our children.'
I touched his face tenderly.
'I understand you mean that,
but we are in a precarious time.
If Zelus or you are captured . . .'

I stopped, not even wanting
to consider or think about it.
I had never seen myself as maternal
until my children were born.
Now they were everything to me.

Before he could answer,
there was a knock and a nymph's voice from
outside our chamber door.
'Styx, Pallas, you are being
summoned before Oceanus.'

I did not know which sister called.
But I knew that if my father
was summoning us both
this late in the night,
something was wrong.

The Darkest Day

As I had been taking care of my own children,
I had not come to the aid of my brothers
in some time. Zelus was older now

but Nike and Kratos were still young enough
to need their mother. To grow into godhood,
the progeny of Gods need a few years.

My children, born as they were during a war,
did not have the luxury of a peaceful upbringing,
and so, as a mother, I did all I could

to shield them from the brutality,
including keeping them in chambers
within this palace where they did not see

their uncles carrying severed heads
and limbs about, bleeding across marble floors.
My mother had only spoken to me once

when she had asked me for more help with the wounded
and I had told her, 'I helped you birth them.
It is your turn to mother them. I have my own

children to think about and tend to.'
But now, as we gathered once again
in Oceanus's grand hall, which was

once known for feasts and now had become
an infirmary where the River Gods healed,
I finally saw the depth and breadth of these attacks.

Once we were all within the hall,
every Oceanid, all the Potamoi,
my father raised his withered old hands.

This war had aged him. He was no longer
the God-King's second-in-command
who threw lush feasts, but a worn father

watching his sons be felled.
His voice, once deep, rich, and vibrant,
now sounded old, ancient, the smallest

of tremors behind each of his words.
'Children,' he began, the word coated
with a sadness as he looked around.

I followed his gaze. All around us were
tired Potamoi, some being held up by Oceanids,
others slouched on the floor, unable to stand.

Pain, an unfamiliar feeling to most Gods,
had become a familiar refrain here.
Their weary spirits were broken.

I had heard my sisters speak of how it was now
taking longer and longer for them to heal.
Even to my own heart, which had turned cold

after the cruel treatment of my siblings,
I found the sight painful to behold.
I looked back to my father as he seemed

to struggle to find his words.
'This has been an extensive, brutal war.
The first and only one of its kind.

For a long time, I thought
that due to our numbers alone,
we would defeat these new Gods,

that they would fall quickly.
After all, these realms have always
been Titan realms.

I have come to the realization,
after many, many nights of ichor
falling like rain from the skies,

of the cries of God after God
shrieking above us, that we . . .'
He paused, looking

so defeated that my heart ached for him.
Was this what mortals had to deal with every day?
Watching their parents grow old before their eyes?

What a cold and brutal fate Kronos had bestowed
upon us, whom he had named his favourites.
It was claimed that his was a golden age.

But as I thought about mortals and their suffering
and looked around this room at our own,
I wondered if there was such a thing

as a golden age at all. Even in times of peace,
Kronos had created a hierarchy, relegating
my sisters and I to nothing but brides and mothers.

My father continued his speech,
turning to Pallas and me.
Something about his gaze gave me pause.

'It is keeping our family in mind,
particularly you, my injured children,
that I have decided the house of Oceanus . . .'

I felt every bone in my being tense.
'The house of Oceanus and Tethys
will no longer participate in this war.'

A Stunned Silence Fell

Shocked, I looked at Pallas.
He stared back at me, not fathoming
what my father could possibly be saying.

Then his brow furrowed; he turned
in the direction of Oceanus.
'My brother Perses leads the Titans,'

his normally gentle voice
quaking with fury I rarely heard.
'I cannot turn my back on my brother.'

My father turned his tired gaze
onto Pallas. 'Then do what you will.
But I cannot watch any more of my children

become injured and imprisoned.'
I stepped next to Pallas, my hands in fists.
'But you are turning your back

on your own brothers. On Perses.
On Asteria.' My voice broke at her name.
Asteria. I had not seen her in so long.

'On their infant daughter Hekate,'
Pallas said quietly, and I let out a sharp hiss,
surprise, sadness, and anger at this revelation.

No one had told me Asteria had had a child.
I had received no word from her in so long.
My heart ached to meet her child, for her to know mine.

Oceanus stared at me for a long moment.
'Your children were meant to herald a change, Styx.
To bring us victory. The prophecy came to me.'

My hackles rose at this. 'Zelus is fighting
as hard as he can. And my other children
are too young to win wars yet.'

My mother, who had been less mother
and more distant guardian to me, said,
'You shield your children too much.

They will grow up to be weak Gods.'
Fury coursed through me at her words.
'I refuse,' I seethed, 'to be a mother

like you. Do you even remember
all our names?' I regretted the words
the moment I spoke them, but it was too late.

I could not take them back.
My father shifted in front of my mother
while Pallas pulled me behind him.

'Enough!' said Oceanus. 'The decision
has been made. We will no longer participate
in this war.' Pallas shook his head

but said nothing. Instead, he wrapped his arm
around my shoulders and led me out of the halls,
as Potamoi and Oceanids alike hurried out of our way.

Pallas's Anger and My Bitterness

made uncomfortable bedfellows.
He was slow to anger, but when he did,

his rage was legendary. Most of it,
he reserved for his forge,

but today, he paced around our chambers.
When Kratos came running in to throw himself

at his legs, Pallas ignored him.
Kratos looked heartbroken.

I tenderly called my son
so I could gather him into me.

He leaned on my shoulder
huffing slightly, keeping tears at bay.

He kept a watchful eye on his father,
unable to understand what he had done wrong.

'I cannot understand why Oceanus
would do this. Without his support,

without the Potamoi, this war is lost!'
I ran my hand through Kratos's

thick curls, so like his father's.
'Perhaps he has finally learned

that his children are more than just weapons.'
Pallas paused and stared at me.

'Styx. Your father treating his children
with value. Do not make me laugh.'

This stung, even though it was the truth.
My parents had seen their countless children

as a way to make themselves more powerful.
But it did not change the fact that they were our parents.

And war changes us all. My father looked older.
Gods should never age, and yet he had

from watching children suffer.
'Do you not think it possible

that all these years of seeing
his children being injured may have

turned him into a kinder God, who longs
for peace for his own family?'

Pallas Finally Stopped Pacing

and approached me on the bed.
He gently touched Kratos's watchful face.

'I know you wish to believe that, Styx,'
he said sorrowfully to me.

'But I think your father is wily enough
to understand we are losing this war.

I think Zeus has made him an offer,
and he has chosen to take it.'

I considered my next words carefully.
'If that is true,' I hesitated, then spoke,

'then my father is not the only one
that Zeus has made such an offer to.'

Pallas's eyes met mine.
'What are you saying?'

I Told Him About Metis's Visit

How she arrived in her gilded glory.
How she looked every inch the God-Queen.
How she had taken my hand and asked
me if I could have goddesshood would I take it?

How taking the side
of the Olympians would guarantee it.
She claimed Zeus was unlike his father,
and how even now, it was not too late.

Not too late to join their side.
How they had a need for Pallas too.
That his weaponry would be mighty
and not like the cumbersome,

poorly made adamantine sword
she wore at her waist now.
When I looked up to meet his eyes,
I saw all of it there.

The sorrow,
the fury,
but worst of all,
the betrayal.

'You promised me' – his voice was hoarse
with a tempered wrath – 'that you would
never keep a secret from me.
Not ever again.'

'And you never kept secrets from me?'
My voice rose sharply.
'Why did you never tell me of Asteria's
daughter, Hekate?'

Pallas ran his hand through his hair,
frustration making his fingers tremble.
'What good would it do for you to know
of a child you may never meet?'

I retreated back from him in revulsion.
'Who are you to make such decisions
for me? She is my niece, my friend's daughter!'

Pallas's eyes met mine and I saw molten fury.
'I am not the one who has kept secrets
that could win or lose us the war!'

My split eyes flashed as I hissed,
'And when was I supposed
to tell you of what happened,
when you are never here?'

My Poniard-shaped Words Made Their Mark

His amber eyes, which I once knew
to hold more warmth than the sun,
looked like the withered petals of a sunflower.

Realizing my own folly, my cruelty,
I reached out to touch his hand.
He evaded my touch.

'Pallas,' I said softly, 'please.'
Kratos, who was asleep now on my lap,
frowned as though he sensed the pain

inside my voice, inside his father's being.
'I did not keep this from you as manipulation.'
Pallas rubbed his face in exhaustion.

'You kept it from me because
you were considering taking the offer,' he said,
his voice edged with a cold fury.

I opened my mouth to protest,
but he was not wrong. Metis had offered me
the one thing I had spent my immortality desiring.

Power.
Recognition.
Goddesshood.

The ability to mould my own destiny.
'I told her no. Despite it all.
I told her *no*.'

Pallas stayed rooted to the spot,
just far enough away from me
so that I could not touch him.

'Your integrity is why I fell in love with you,'
he told me, his voice softening slightly.
'The way you refused to bow down

to the fate you were given, no matter
how unfair your father and Kronos were.
No matter how cruel your siblings.

I fell in love with you because I thought you knew.'
I paused and stared into his eyes, not fathoming.
'What did you think I knew?'

Pallas gazed at me, his features betraying surprise.
'That you were already powerful, Styx.
You do not need to be a Goddess.'

I let out a cold, bitter laugh at this.
'Pallas. Do you not understand how that sounds?
You are already a God. What do you know

about being relegated to nurse and bride?
What do you know about being only a vessel
to carry Gods into existence, but never

being allowed the status or power of one?'
Pallas looked at me as though seeing
me for the very first time.

Then he said quietly, 'I will not betray my brother.
Not even for you, Styx. I will not do it.'
He turned and began to walk away.

'Wait,' I called to him, my hand on Kratos's hair,
soothing both him and myself.
'You should know a truth before you leave.'

He stopped, but refused to turn around.
I opened my mouth and hated
the tremor that was rooted there.

'We are to have another child.'
This was not how I wanted to tell him.
He had been overjoyed when I had told him

about Kratos and Nike. But this day
felt like there was a chasm between us.
He stood there silently for an age.

Finally, he said to me, 'Send word
when the infant arrives.'
And with those cold words, he left.

I knew without premonition
that something between us had changed.
And that this chasm would only widen.

Gods Had Never Had Reason to Count Days Before

but now, time took
on a different meaning.
Time meant more injuries.

Time meant returning
to battle after healing,
only to come home injured again.

Time meant children born
and fathers unable to be
present at their births.

No one will ever tell you
that the meaning of time
changes when you are within a war.

If you are immortal,
it does not even end in death,
just a battle that rages on and on forever.

I gave birth to Bia alone,
with only Nike to aid me.
I sent word to Pallas, and received no response.

I understood his anger at me. But why at Bia?
My child of force and courage was my easiest birth.
Already she was her brother and sister's most beloved.

Watching my three youngest children bond
as Kratos and Nike took turns holding their sister
brought me more joy that I thought imaginable.

When I finally received word from Pallas,
it was only to tell me that Kratos, like Zelus,
was required on the Titan front.

I seethed. I had already given one son to this war.
Kratos had only just become old enough
to own his godhood, and now he was required

to bleed ichor for his kin who barely knew him.
I refused to send an answer back.
If Pallas wanted him, he would have to

go through me. No more children of mine
were going to be sacrificed to this senseless war,
not whilst they lived in my home.

When the second messenger from Pallas arrived,
I did not even go to greet him.
Instead, I stayed in my chambers

playing with Bia. Nights passed before
it finally happened. My worst fears realized.
Thunder and lightning flashed across the sky

when the chamber doors were flung open.
Pallas, his clothes drenched in golden blood,
amber eyes wide, stood. In his arms

was our oldest son, Zelus. Both his arms
had been cut off. And a messenger behind them
was holding them. I could not help it.

In my grief, I screamed.

A Mother's Rage

I had always said Zelus was too young.
He had not enjoyed a long childhood
as he should, and when he was barely old enough,
he had been stationed with his uncle Perses
leading a war front he was not ready for.

I had been terrified this time would come.
Pallas looked into my eyes, his own wide
with shock. My chest hurt as I saw
our son was not even conscious,
that Pallas could barely carry him.

'Bring him inside!' I told him urgently,
taking Zelus's arms from the messenger.
How could this have happened to my son?
Pallas had promised.
He had *PROMISED*.

Pallas laid Zelus on the bed and I
instantly got to work. My old spells,
my old herbs in hand,
I first soothed his wounds
and cast a spell for his pain.

Then, using the sacred thread Asteria and I
made long before the war to stitch
the wound of one of my River God brothers,
whom Metis had clawed to within an inch of his life,
I stitched his arms back on.

My tears fell freely
as I watched his face for winces of pain.
When I was done, covered in my child's

blood, I turned to Pallas. '*How . . .*
How did this happen?'

He was sitting on the edge of the bed,
his face in his hands. 'It . . . it was my fault.
I let Perses take him too far into the fray.
Poseidon and Hades came for him.
He could not handle both at once.'

My hands turned into fists.
'You told me nothing would happen
to our children. You promised!'
Pallas looked at me in anguish.
'Styx, I did everything I could.

It's war and there was—'
I raised a hand to stop him.
'I do not wish to hear it.
My child is injured, he will take
some time to heal. It is best you leave.'

But Pallas did not move.
'We need Kratos to take Zelus's place.'
I could not believe what I was hearing.
'*No.*'
The word was edged in poison.

'Styx—' Pallas began.
'I told you,' I said quietly,
'I will sacrifice no more children
to this war. Not while my son
lies there maimed.'

I had to keep my children safe.
I had to shield them. I stared at Pallas.
He had failed to protect our son.
So now it was my duty alone
to defend my children.

'You failed me,' I told him coldly.
'You failed our family.
I will now do what I must do.
And you will not question
my decision.'

Pallas's grief-stricken face
was frozen for an age.
It was as though a thousand
silent words passed between us.
And then he slowly nodded.

Olympus

The invitation came not long after
I had sent my own messenger.

As Oceanus's palace now no longer
contained Gods fighting the Olympians,

Metis herself escorted us to Zeus.
In her time at war, Metis's might

had only grown. She could harness
the winds at whim in a way

neither Asteria nor I
could ever have mastered.

We had all underestimated her,
and it was our own undoing.

To Pallas and I, and our children,
Metis only smiled.

She embraced me and said tenderly,
'You have made the right choice.

Do not doubt that.
Zeus will treat you and yours well.'

A darkness unsettled me still,
but to Metis I offered a tight smile

as she harnessed the winds again
and we stepped, seemingly, into air.

'The journey is not long,'
Metis reassured us all.

As we flew together into the clouds,
it was Bia who first saw it.

'Mother, look!' And there it was.
The mighty white pillars of Mount Olympus.

The palaces were built with adamantine
to protect them from harm,

and the smoothest marble I had ever seen,
to hide them in the clouds

from wandering Titan eyes.
The residences were built in a circle;

the centre held the dome of the Gods.
Two golden thrones sat in the middle,

one for Zeus and one for Metis.
Around them were more thrones

for the other Olympian Gods.
It was a marvel to behold.

When we arrived, Zeus rose
from his throne and walked toward us,

arms open in greeting.
'Welcome, sisters and brothers,

I am delighted you have accepted
my offer. You are well met.'

Zeus

The stories that were told of him
in hushed voices by the Potamoi
had revealed that he was a terrible foe.

That his thunderbolts were more
powerful than adamantine.
That his heart was made of stone.

That he and his brothers and sisters
had turned our Titan siblings into
a sea of limbs and heads easily.

Their bloodlust seemed unquenchable,
and they wanted power at any cost.
I did not trust them.

Not after what they had done to my son.
But I knew that we would not win
and I knew what would happen

to the side that lost this war.
And that fate . . . that fate was not one
I wanted for my family.

So I did what I had to.
I smiled at Zeus at best I could
and said, 'We are honoured to be here.'

Fate

As we sat in audience with Zeus,
we were offered ambrosia and nectar.

Our children drank and ate happily,
but Pallas and I declined any offerings.

We were still tense, unsure of the cost.
'Pallas,' Zeus's voice boomed,

'we would like you to start crafting
weapons for us. We could use your mastery.'

Pallas did not say anything,
just gave the slightest of nods.

Then Zeus turned to my children.
Only Nike, Kratos, and Bia had joined us.

Zelus was still healing in our chambers.
'As for you, you will join us in battle, yes?'

I tensed at this, my back straightening.
'No. That wasn't in the agreement.' I pulled Bia close.

Zeus frowned. 'Metis, did you not mention it?'
Metis simply smiled. 'I thought it would be

better coming from you, my king.'
How had I never noticed her catlike

features, her sly feline smile as she turned
whole rooms to her favour?

'We ask all Gods who join us
to fight, Styx,' Zeus told me.

'Your father was allowed otherwise,
because he simply offered to reduce

the Titan forces by three thousand Gods.'
I stared at him. 'But Bia is only young.'

I looked down at my smallest child.
The others were almost full-grown Gods now.

Zeus was quiet. 'I see. Well, we can allow
Bia more time to grow older.

But if the war still continues,
she must join us. Our numbers

are less that the Titans.
They can keep their Goddesses home.

We need our Goddesses
to fight alongside us.'

I waited. Waited for Pallas to say something,
for Metis to reproach Zeus.

But when none of them spoke,
I took a long, deep breath.

'No.' The word was quiet,
holding my every conviction.

Zeus leaned forward,
and I saw the cold in his features.

‘I think you are mistaken, nymph,
about what you get to dictate here.’

My body felt like it had turned to ice,
but I stood my ground.

‘My children are not a bargaining chip
for any God, mighty Zeus.’

He sat back, his features betraying
a growing fury that I felt upon me.

‘It is either this or when I win,
and I will win, make no mistake,

you and your daughters will be enslaved.
Your consort and sons will be in cages.

Your choice, nymph.
Either they fight for us now,

or you all spend an eternity
I will ensure is an absolute agony.’

The brutality and finality in his words
made my own fury give way to

something I had never felt before.
Fear. Fear for my daughters. My sons.

For Pallas. I could take any punishment
Zeus meted on me. But not my children.

Not Pallas. Realizing I had no choice left,
I accepted defeat bitterly with these words,

'You promise nothing
will harm my children?'

And Zeus smiled.
The smile of a shark seeing prey.

'I promise. They will be protected.'

A Visitor

Only Bia and I returned
to my father's palace.
Pallas, Nike, and Kratos
stayed in Olympus
to discuss battle plans.

As Nyx painted the sky dark,
I realized that Zeus had not
promised *me* anything,
no mention of goddesshood.
But as I watched Zelus heal,

his body finally coming back
together, painfully, slowly,
it occurred to me that
as long as my children
were safe from imprisonment,

from an eternity of pain like this,
I did not need any promises
from anyone. My own ambitions
were a small price to pay
for the safety of my children.

I felt weary.
But then on the balcony
came a flash of light. For a moment,
fear seized me,
thinking it was Zeus.

Instead, when the light passed,
I saw the figure wasn't a God.
It was Asteria holding

in her hand the last
embers of a falling star.

My heart leaped at the sight of her.
I stepped out onto the balcony,
my eyes glistening with tears.
I had missed her deeply,
even though I had tried not to.

Eras without her had been
so hard to bear. Her own eyes
spilled over with tears as she whispered,
'Styx.' We embraced
and I remembered

all those days when we were girls.
Everything we had made together,
from the eels to the starfox,
eons ago, and yet those memories
were the happiest of my life.

I realized then as I felt her body hold mine,
how motherhood had changed us both.
'Asteria,' I said quietly,
pulling back to take a look at her,
'I heard you had a child.'

Betrayal

In a happier time, we would have been
together through each child's birth,
as we had promised each other
all those years ago, our naivety stemming
from an immortality that had never known
war, destruction, pain.

Torn apart by this conflict,
we had missed so much of each other's lives.
Perses and Pallas had still got to see each other
through the wars, but we had been kept apart
all this time. Goddesses and nymphs were forbidden
to leave our homes for we may be captured.

I smiled and kissed her cheek.
'I hear her name is Hekate.
She must be just as extraordinary as you are.'
I did not ask where Hekate was. I knew.
Asteria had taken a great risk to see me.
If she had been seen, she would have been seized.

Asteria smiled back, but then her face dropped.
'Styx, Perses says we will not win this war.
Since your father withdrew
the River Gods, our numbers have fallen.'
I was quiet. I knew these words well now.
So instead I listened.

'And . . . and Perses told me today
that Pallas has . . . that you have—'
Her eyes filled with grief now.
'Is it true that you have chosen
the side of the Olympians?'
I looked away, unable to meet her eye.

'Asteria. We had to. Zelus . . .'
I gestured to her to follow and led her
into my chambers to show her
the still-healing body of my son.
She gasped, her hand moving
to her mouth in horror.

'This palace has been full
of injured Gods just like him.
My brothers have borne the brunt
of this war,' I said softly.
'It's their pain that convinced
my father to withdraw.'

Asteria's hands trembled
as she touched my son's forehead.
'Have you given him—'
I nodded. 'Yes, the potion we made.'
I smiled wryly. 'It is working.'
She turned to me, her eyes wide.

'We could use them, Styx,'
she said urgently, 'Our powers.
Our skills. We could use them
the way Metis has helped
the Olympians.'
I frowned at her words.

'We promised each other we wouldn't,'
I reminded her. 'And I do not think

I possess the same talent as Metis,
Asteria. She has powerful, stranger gifts.'
Asteria shook her head.
'No, Styx, she just had practice.'

'Do you know what both
the Titans and the Olympians
would do if they learned
what we can do, Asteria?'
I challenged her.
'Styx, we must try,' Asteria pleaded.

I stared at the sleeping form of my son,
then back at my dearest friend.
'If you want to do what is best
for your infant daughter, Asteria,
do not do this. Do what you can
to protect your child.'

Asteria stepped back from me.
'As you have done?' she asked in pain.
'By betraying your own?'
My eyes narrowed.
'I did what I had to so
my children could be safe.'

The colour drained from her face.
'Perses leads the Titan army,'
she said, grief lacing her words.
'Does it not occur to you
that perhaps I *cannot* surrender?
That perhaps we do not have

the luxury of choice?'
I trembled with fury and guilt
at her words. 'Do you think,'
I hissed at her, 'that this was easy

for me? That I chose this lightly?'
Asteria glared at me now.

'You got to choose, Styx.
This is what I mean.'
In my anger, I turned away
from her and said,
'I did what I had to
for those I love.'

Asteria's voice, soft and shaking,
was almost a whisper when she said,
'Once, a long time ago,
you loved me too.'
My heart broke. I turned
to look at her, to answer,

but she was gone.

If I Had Known

that it was one of the last times
I would ever see her,
I would have held her longer.

I would have tried to persuade her.
I would have hidden her in our palace.
I would have hidden Hekate here too.

But back then,
I felt betrayed.
I felt unending grief.

I was furious she had chosen
to side with the losing Titans,
just as she was sorrowful

I had changed allegiance to the Olympians.
A family split in two is still a family.
We had just lost sight of it all.

So much ichor had fallen now.
So much blood had been shed.
When the news came

that the Titans who still fought Zeus
were being captured,
their weapons falling useless

against his thunderbolts,
that Titan lands were no match
for Poseidon's floods and hurricanes,

that Hera's birds knew too many
Titan secrets for the older Gods to win,
I knew that I chose right

for my children.
Still, my heart broke
for Asteria and Hekate.

The Aftermath of War

When Nyx's night spread darkness for days on end, Nike returned home to tell me it was almost over. She wove a tale so sordid that my very bones hurt to hear it. She said that Gaia, upset at her own children, the Titans, had chosen to help her youngest grandchildren, the Olympians, instead. Gaia told Zeus every secret we had kept so guarded. Where our palaces were, where stores of adamantine lay, how to convince Oceanus to withdraw his many children from battle. Where we ached most. Our weak points. The idea that a mother could turn on her own children that way felt like anathema to me. But then, I was her first grandchild, and she had never had a kind word for me. Her words had been true. I was not beautiful. This had caused me more trouble, more pain in my immortal life than necessary. Now, Nike told me of the cages my own consort Pallas had built to hold the Titan generals. My uncle Hyperion was one of them. Zeus had asked Hyperion's son Helios, who had turned on the Titans, to take over his father's duties. All this time I thought Gods were irreplaceable. And look how easy it was to even replace the God who lifted the sun into the sky. The worst of the fates was in store for gentlehearted Atlas, who fought so fiercely and powerfully for us. Zeus decreed that it was his punishment to hold the heavens upon his shoulders forever. A burden that would never end. 'What of the rest?' I asked Nike. Her once sweet face now held a bitterness I did not recognize. War had changed her too. 'You must go to Olympus to see their fates, mother,' she said quietly. 'Zeus wants us all there for when it ends. *Every one of us.*'

A Ceremony

It was the opposite of a feast.
The remaining Titans gathered,
but there was no joy, no chatter.

We knew what was coming.
When I finally saw Pallas again,
he did not hold me nor I him.

We barely acknowledged each other.
Zelus came with me, now that
he was mended. Gold scars

seared across his arms where
I had stitched them back.
Bia, her Goddess in full bloom,

joined us at the centre of Mount Olympus,
as did Nike and Kratos.
My children seemed distant,

different somehow from
how I had raised them.
Only sweet Bia held my hand

and stayed by my side.
Next to Zeus's throne were
wretched adamantine cages

holding Gods soaked in their own ichor,
defeated and broken.
My uncles, once so proud.

Pallas and Perses's own father, Crius.
Asteria's father, Coeus.
My heart ached for the two elder Gods

who had only shown me kindness.
I remembered their smiling faces.
Now they sat huddled behind bars.

I looked away, unable to see this.
It was a stripping of dignity.
And in that moment, I could only think

how grateful I was that neither
my father nor Pallas
were in those cruel cages.

With a pang of love, I glanced at my consort,
but he refused to look at me,
his eyes gazing at the cage

his own hands had built for his father.
It was as though all the warmth
had been drained from his body.

All Titans seemed duller now.
I noticed that none of the Titanides
were there. My heart thumped

What had happened to them.
Finally, Zeus spoke.
'Friends!
Welcome!

And be glad you chose
the side that was victorious
for it could be you in these cages.'

He used his thunderbolt
to smack at Coeus's cage.
The old God jolted.

I blinked back tears.
It was in his palace I had spent
so much of my childhood.

'First, we will give gifts
to those who joined us.
Your loyalty has not gone unnoticed.

To the Titan Gods. Your realms
will be smaller, your powers fewer,
but you will still rule parts of your worlds.'

Some gift this was.
To have less and lose family
felt like a pyrrhic victory.

Zeus continued,
his eyes roving over us
until they landed on me.

'Every nymph who stood with us
is now to be a Water Goddess.
Their realms the sea or river.'

Ah. So this was why I saw
some of my sisters here,
Amphitrite, Doris, Clymene.

Perhaps there had been more
Oceanids who had chosen like me than I had realized.
'But for Styx, whose consort

Pallas has been essential to our victory,
and her children Zelus, Nike,
and Kratos so powerful on our side,

I anoint her, The River,
whose waters every God
must swear an oath to.

She will be the great river
who tends to the dead
as their souls come to the Underworld.

Her name will be on the lips
of every God, of every mortal.
She will be revered and feared by all.'

Is It Still Called Victory If No One Celebrates It?

Neither my children's faces
nor Pallas's face lit up for me.

My sisters did not seem
to delight in their wins either.

Instead, we all stood stoic and still,
our eyes on Zeus. A palpable fear

rose amongst the tired Titans
as he turned his attention

to the Titan generals
he held in the cages.

'Every Titan who stood against me' –
his voice was cold and callous –

'will be taken to Tartarus.'
This we had expected.

But what he said next
devastated every one of us.

'You may have wondered why we chose
Olympus as our seat of power.

This mountain sits atop
the deepest of Tartarus's caverns.

We have asked a favour from the old God:
He says he will help us with these treacherous Titans.

Their leader, Perses, has already
been taken down and tied to the side of the cavern.'

He pointed to the marble floors
of Olympus. As we watched,

a strange thing happened.
Tendrils of gold rose from inside

the marble, and like ivy,
began to take over the floor.

'Each Titan God who stood against me,'
Zeus said coldly. 'Their ichor

will be used to turn this mountain into gold.'

My Chest Felt Hollow

Under our feet,
the blood of Perses was turning
the white marble floors of Olympus
into ichor gold. A reminder
of everything we had lost.

I turned to look at Pallas.
His eyes were closed in pain,
his jaw clenched tight.
I reached for his hand, but he flinched.

I knew he blamed me for this.
But this would have been our sons' fates,
his fate too. Could he not see that?
I did what I could to save them all.

But Zeus was not finished.
He turned to those of us gathered.
'As for the Titanides, the wives
and daughters of these Titans' –

he paused to look at his brother
Poseidon and they both smirked –
'to the victor go the spoils.'
My heart froze.

A cry resounded across Olympus:
'NO!' It was so hoarse and broken
I almost did not realize that the voice . . .
the word . . . it was mine.

'You Object, Styx?'

There was a dangerous edge to Zeus's voice.
But I had faced a powerful God
and protested his decisions before.

I stepped forward and said,
'Leave the Titanides alone.
They did not fight against you.'

Zeus's eyes turned thunderous.
'But they did. They stayed loyal
to husbands and sons and fathers

who stood against us. That is
a declaration enough.'
I shook my head.

'Many did not have a choice.'
Zeus walked in my direction
and I felt Pallas's eyes on me.

I knew what he was thinking.
If Zeus decided to punish me
for speaking against him,

there would be nothing he could do.
But Zeus instead put his hand
on my shoulder and said,

'They all had a choice, Styx.
Just as you did. And you chose correctly.'
I grimaced at his fingers touching me.

I wanted to claw at them till he removed
his unwanted grip on my shoulder.
But instead, I said calmly,

'You said you would not be like your father.'
Before I could stop myself, I continued,
'But do you not see how this is worse?'

Zeus gave me a smile, but there was
no warmth in it. Instead, he boomed,
'Let me show you how I am better

than my father ever was.
You, Styx, will have the goddesshood
you always desired. For your poisonous tongue,

your bitterness, your capacity to turn
on those you claim to love so easily . . .
I name you the Goddess of Hatred.'

My inside felt like it was wilting.
I stared at Zeus, my fury and humiliation
rendering me unable to speak.

He continued, 'But look, there is more.
Your children, powerful, brilliant
as they are, will stay here on Olympus.

My most exalted warriors,
deified forever as my own.'
A hum rose from the collected Titans.

But I knew very well what Zeus was doing.
My children were *too* powerful.
He was separating them from me,

the one who had openly showed
she would stand against him
in defence of fallen Titanides.

To separate a family
is to have power over it.
My children were to be taken from me.

For I had dared
to defy
a God-King.

The Three Realms

I could barely see through my grief
as I heard the three brothers,
Zeus, Poseidon, and Hades,
divide the three realms between them.

Zeus got the sky.
Poseidon, the sea.
And Hades, the Underworld.
Looking at Hades and the tales

that were spun of him during
the Titanomachy, it was hard
to believe this young God,
who looked scarcely more than a boy,

was capable of the cruelty he committed in war.
But I had learned over the long arc
of this war that we were all capable
of terrible things. We were all

fate's own folly. It did not matter
if we were Gods or mortals.
Hades came to me, his long raven hair
almost beautiful as it reflected Helios's sun.

He bowed, his dark robes swishing.
'Styx,' he said quietly, 'I promise you
that I will not interfere in your work.
Your river is your realm.

I will have no say over it.
But know this, other than Pallas,
all other Gods and Goddesses
can only visit the Underworld

with my permission.'
Out of the three brothers,
I was surprised to find Hades
the most tolerable, with his respectful manner

a small consolation in the grief I felt
upon losing my children.
I turned to look at Zeus, wishing my glare
was powerful enough to destroy a God-King.

I noticed finally that Metis
was nowhere to be seen.
'Where is Metis?' I whispered.
'Did you not know what happened?'

Hades's words held a strange succour to them,
almost as though he felt pity for me.
'She defied Zeus. So he devoured her.'
My whole body felt like it was breaking.

I turned to Hades and whispered,
'He devoured her?' Hades nodded slowly.
'I am sorry, Styx. Hera is said to be
Zeus's next God-Queen.'

For all Metis's powers,
for all her talents,
she could not fight Zeus.
'H-how did she defy him?' I asked.

'I do not know precisely,
but Zeus said she could do things

no Goddess should be able to do.'
Hades frowned. 'I do not know what

he meant by these words.'
But I did. I knew what he meant.
He meant her magic made her terrifying.
He meant he was afraid of her stranger powers.

Powers both Asteria and I had.
That no God knew we could hold.
And I promised myself that to keep
my children who were hostage here safe,

I would never use the powers
that scared a God-King.
I would never practise magic
or spellwork again.

A Final Act

I held my children so close.
Bia wept uncontrollably.
Nike could barely hold her tears
back when I let her go.

Kratos, my sweet boy, whispered,
'When we have permission,
we will visit, Mother.'
Zelus walked with us

until the gates of Olympus
stopped him from going any farther.
I turned back to look at him,
his sad eyes watching us go.

Pallas and I returned to Oceanus's palace.
Our chambers felt empty.
After years of children that I had raised
it was only the two of us again.

A wide abyss had been crafted
between us. One made of war.
Broken vows.
Betrayal.

Pallas turned to me.
'Styx,' he said quietly,
his voice rough with brokenness,
'please look at me.'

I looked into his eyes.
He skimmed his fingers
along my jawline.

'I know why you chose this.
I know now, it was not
just for you. It was for us.
You wanted us to be spared

the fate that . . . that . . .'
He could not finish.
But I shook my head bitterly.
'I failed, Pallas.

He took our children.'
Pallas shook his head.
'You did not fail.
We are not in cages.'

He pulled me close,
into his arms, and I realized then
my inability to feel anything.
It was as though my love

had curdled. Zeus's decree
had taken all my warmth
from me. I could only feel
a faint echo of any love I once had.

I had turned into something else.
'He has made me a monster, Pallas,'
I whispered hoarsely.
'You should . . . you do not have to

be with me if you do not want.'
Pallas tilted my chin up
so that our eyes met.
'I will always love you.

Nymph. Goddess. Monster.
My love for you will remain.'

His lips brushed mine
and he kissed me deeply.

Perhaps hate had not yet
destroyed every part of me,
for I kissed him back with as much
fervour as the first time eons ago.

Before I Left

I had something I needed to do.
One final act of sisterhood.

One final act of defiance
to Zeus. I searched for a messenger.

I found one hiding in the cave
Asteria and I had once loved so much.

He was wearing Perses's seal.
He was injured, but his wings still worked.

I took his hand, gave him the last potent
healing potion that I had made before the decree.

'You must fly to Perses's palace,'
I whispered softly.

'You must tell Asteria and Hekate
that the war is lost. They must run.'

The messenger stared at me,
his brown eyes confused,

but at my grim face,
his eyes widened and he nodded.

Within moments of my spell,
he had healed enough to go.

I watched his form in the sky
flying to Perses's palace.

If nothing else,
it would give them a chance.

A chance to *run*.

River of the Dead

To be powerful after years of no power.
To be given goddesshood after years
of simply being a nymph
was a cataclysm of emotions.

Here in the Underworld,
no sisters defied me,
no brothers called me names.
No father tried to barter me,

and no mother used me for my skills.
I tended to the dead, their spirits silver
inside my waters as I took each one
and guided it to where it must go.

The ferryman, Charon, was as quiet
as he was kind. And Hades was true
to his word. He never came between me
and my work. I grew to love the silence here.

This mouth of the Underworld
where my river flowed from
almost resembled the cavern
that Asteria and I spent our girlhoods in.

Asteria. I thought about her often.
About her sister and her mother.
I had heard Phoebe and Leto served
at Zeus's leisure. Poseidon too

held many Titanides hostage.
Hades was the best of three brothers.
He had not taken a single Titanide
and he stayed within his realm.

Pallas and I were closer now.
The chasm between us slowly healing.
It would never be fully healed,
but we were both learning different ways to love

inside this strange place.
Perhaps this ending was hard won.
But in ending there is a beginning.
And in beginnings there is hope of a new dawn.

Epilogue

When I was born, my grandmother prophesied
that I would not be beautiful,

and that this would mean I would lack power.
My grandmother was wrong.

It was true that I was not beautiful,
but my lack of beauty led me to carve

my own way into power.
I fought and found my own paths.

I did not need to be pretty
to become the dread river of oaths.

I did not need to be beautiful
to mother four powerful Gods.

I clawed my way from nymph
to Goddess all by myself.

And yes, the losses have been great.
Grief has made a home within me.

But the power is mine for good now.
Once my sisters laughed at me,

deemed themselves better than I could ever be,
but I am my own potent story of rage and tragedy.

Now I hear footsteps beyond my cave,
someone is following my river in the Underworld.

I hear the sound of a mother and a daughter
walking toward me.

I know who they are.
Asteria, Titan queen.

And her daughter, the beacon of Titan hope.
Hekate.

Acknowledgments

As with *Hekate*, *Styx* came to me as a dream. I knew, however, that this story could not be told through a single point of view. Not when Asteria was Styx's only solace and friend. And as it is with friends as well as books, it takes a village to support an author.

To Steve, who has stood by me through every word, every worry big or small and who has always known precisely what I need, precisely when I need it. Thank you for holding my hand and not letting go.

To my agent Niki Chang who has always been my champion and the best agent I could have asked for, thank you endlessly for believing in my work.

To David Evans and Emmanuel Omodeinde for looking after me through the ever-changing and river like process of editing this book.

To Charlotte Trumble, for being so tender with Styx and Asteria's story and for such an incredible editorial journey, thank you! To Margaret Raymo, for your generous edits, your patience and holding Styx and Asteria's story with the love and care it needed, thank you!

To lovely Gemma Creffield and wonderful Samantha Gentry for fearlessly taking over the reins – I cannot wait to keep working with you both!

To my dear friends Elodie Harper and Jennifer Saint, none of this trilogy would exist without your encouragement, your compassion, your generosity. I am blessed to know such brilliance as you!

To Micaela Alcaino, I will forever tell people the story of how fortunate I am to be working with you – thank you for saying yes to this project and making such gorgeous covers for both *Hekate* and now *Styx*!

To the wonderful team at Simon and Schuster UK and the amazing team at Little Brown Young Readers, you continue to be my beacons of light and hope – thank you for giving this project so much love and for being on this powerful journey with me!

To all my fellow practitioners and daughters of Hellenic paganism – your guidance and love has made this trilogy stronger. Thank you.

To lovely Natalie Haynes, thank you for being a light for us all and your continued excellence as a writer and my friend. Adore you!

With deepest of gratitude to Sweety, Anita, Dean, Niall, Carlos, Yrsa, Costanza, Bea, Rosie, Alwyn, Rowan, Lucy, Trista, Ben, Anne, Laurie, Alison, Shaun, Rebekah, Clara, Annie, my parents and my brother.

And finally to you, dear reader. Thank you so much for entering the world of the River Styx with me. Thank you for taking the more difficult waters and opening your heart to her story. May hope and kindness always find you where you are.